THIS BOOK IS DEDICATED TO THE DEATHLESS MEMORY OF

PAULA & JOSÉ VEGA
&
YOLANDA VEGA TORRES

Serena

or,
THE NIGHT AIR.

BEING A MOST DEFTLY
WRITTEN
Florilegium, Compendium
&
Offertory Garland
OF
These Distracted Times.

✠

WRITTEN BY
The Most Eminent
SCRIBE & SERVANT
MR JOSEPH GALVÁN.

MMXXII

ADVERTISEMENT.

☞THE AUTHOR OF THE FOREGOING BOOK, though being of limited MEANS, & availing Himſelf by the *Sovereign Pow'r* of ALMIGHTY GOD, now wishes to thank the following *August* Perſons for *their moſt generous Succour* in creating this WORK:

Robert Everſmann
Mickey Collins
Taylor Pope
Sara Kachelman
Raveena Bhalara
Shannon Edwardſ
Kaſie Shahbaz
Diana Sharp
Andrew Shaw-Kitch
Alex Behr
Klint Finley
Karina Agbiſit
Harper Quinn
Iſaac Yoder
Margaret Malone
Daniela del Mar
Iſaac Lewis
Maddiſon Bond
Chris Aſhby
Charley Locke
Daniel Gumbiner and
Jonny Shewell

The AUTHOR wiſhes eſpecially to thank hiſ MOTHER, MISS MARGARET CAMACHO for Her *unfailing* LOVE & GUIDANCE.

Table of Contents

King of Cups

I AM THE KING OF CUPS. IN MY RIGHT HAND I bear a chalice. In this chalice, a fish is speaking to me. I have been timeless, alive for hundreds of years in this, my palace of tides. The water surrounding it is clear, clear as aquamarine and cold as ice. The water is whatever you like to call it. I bear the cup. I distill the waters of Lethe, the waters of oblivion, through which all men pass. In me is past, present and future. I am the king of cups, ruler of the fens of eternity, prince of the tidelands, master and admiral of the ocean sea.

From my palace I have seen the moon turn over in her sphere countless times. I have watched the planets align in syzygy. I have many times witnessed the sun eclipse itself in a perfect black sphere from my throne of morganite and spring water. In my obsidian and amethyst palace I am the king of the greater and lesser waters. Emeralds line my throne of shocked quartz. Water lilies nod dreamlessly in the pools of my courtyard. My fountains spout and gush abundantly in my garden. My royal dais is a cushion of jasmine petals, watered silk, leafy green reeds, damask cloth, royal indigo divans. Blue delphiniums spring at my footfalls. In my palace, water floods the marble floors and spills down the white steps.

Sereno

Fountain nymphs linger in the cool wet shade of box hedge and cool dewy grass. The ivy-covered walls drip fat drops of sweet rain. My chamber is a bathhouse, my harem a steam room, my boudoir a waterbed.

Drink from my chalice. Drink from me. Drink me deep. Feel me course inside you. Feel my clean cold water course down your parched and aching throat. Feel me settle in you, feel my waters blossom inside you, churn in you, cool your bilious humours.

Today I opened the Book of Time. In a caravel once I traversed the Sea of Memories. One day I arrived in Lisbon to watch the Marquês of Pombal expel the Jesuits. From there, I traveled to Calicut and watched some Konkani men haul a magnificent giant baroque pearl from the milky sea. I went to Dili and sipped warm coconut milk with the Sultan of Brunei. I dipped macaroons in melted white chocolate in Jakarta under a palace of palm fronds and ylang-ylang. My nose caught a whiff of the fragrance of clove and cinnamon from an island in the Java Sea. I travelled to Lisbon in my caravel with white sails and disembarked at Nagasaki when the peonies were in full bloom, and the moon shone on the black waters at Dejima. At Delphi I gathered, from the waters of the Castalian spring, the holy ichor that once flowed from the heights of Parnassus. In the *Hagiasma* of St Mary in Constantinople, I drank from the ice-cold turquoise water formed by the tears of the Virgin of Mercy, and luxuriated with Suleyman in Topkapi on his bed of rose petals and orange blossoms. Through time and space I have traversed this ocean of desire, have set sails for the western paradise, have stomped through wetlands that stretched to the horizon, have traced my way through box canyons and windbreaks of cypress. I have dined with kings and mystics, have raised crystal goblets to toast the dying world around me. In my palace are hangings of blue silk the color of the sky and the raiment of the Virgin; she tossed her girdle to me once, and entranced by her favor, I watched as it floated through the sky and landed in my garden of water hyacinth and blue lobelias.

You know me. We have seen one another. You may have seen me on the street, looking at you as you passed by, hoping to be unnoticed, wanting to be forgotten. Was it perhaps one day in Mexico City 1904 that you watched the rain sluice down the tiles of the cathedral and form wide puddles that the street vendors rustled their carts through? You watched me from the window through a drawn shade in that palace of lava rock and veneered wood. Or maybe you found me in Florence beside a stone cherub at I Tatti in 1939, as the world was coming to an end but the land rolled out as it did when Medici men enticed dancing boys in their palazzos with flacons of wine and marzipan phalli. You saw me with the British rolling ashore on D-Day, or you saw me at Bad Kissingen warding off the Stasi. You saw me, ancient and dewy-eyed, in my temple at Warm Springs, in the crescent moon in a heaven of pink clouds, in Nergal of Innana-Sin, in the rock face of Meribah, struck by Moses to chide the Israelites for their unbelief. When Jesus healed the man at Bethesda, the angel who stirred the waters saw me first.

I am deathless and ageless. I am the King of the Overflowing Chalice, I who saw Christ and Cæsar, Agrippa and Aristotle, Buddha and Boudicca. I am the King of Cups, who on a shallop in Xochimilco four-hundred years ago beckoned Sor Juana to write a hymn to the Holy Sacrament. In my palace of crystal, my palace of watered silk, filled with pillows that float in a flooded chamber covered in ivy and jasmine, in my hall of flamingoes and palms, my chapel of desire, I call to you like the lover that I am, I beckon to you. You have seen me at the foot of your bed, beckoning to you to open the Book of Time with me, to ascend the steps of my palace, to greet me with a warm and watery kiss.

Drink from my chalice of warm memories; imbibe the essence of love, let this gift run through you like a river, until your body, drunk with longing, drops noiselessly into the pool of dreams.

It is I who am telling you these stories. It is I who am telling them to you as you sleep. When you wake and you write them down, you are only able to do so because in the twilight of your sleep, we drank together.

Come join me. Come to the silence. Come listen to the still waters of this, your palace. Come and refresh your body in my placid, pure waters. Come and dream endlessly with me on a sparkling raft made of starlight, quetzal feathers, fog, and diamond tears.

Sereno

Osmanthus & White Pepper

SOMETIMES I SEE YOU AT THE FOOT OF MY bed. I can see your figure emerge from the dark and fall into the bars of light falling through the windowpanes above my dresser, and I can see you, clear as day, in your jean jacket and waffle henley, your joggers, your toboggan covering your head, your hazel eyes, your lips, the stubble that marked where your mustache used to be. The tears come then, they form in the corners of my eyes and roll down my cheeks and over the hairs of my beard there in the dark. I cry for a few minutes before I lull myself back into sleep. I have to forget about you. I have to keep moving forward.

You always recede into the dark. Every night you appear like this, the smoke dissipates slowly but deliberately, like a scud cloud that accompanies the low ragged rains of October over the hills in Portland. I still feel the cold embrace of your fingers in mine, the smell of cheap beer and the feel of rough denim, the free-wheeling airs of your conversation, that glare, that toothy smile, those long slender pale fingers, that scrawl on Post-Its. I keep these relics in a cardboard box under my cast-iron bed: a packet of postcards you wrote in Prague filled with brain vomit and self-hate, a pallet of unending anxiety and wild-eyed rollicking depression. Each of these postcards reads like a razor-blade drawn over skin. But I read them over and over again, self-indulgent, as if St John Nepomucene himself relayed these secrets from his basilica, wrote them out on the Charles Bridge, stamped them, and sent them to me.

But it could not be that I don't want you to stop visiting. No. I don't want you to stop appearing to me in your nimbus of white orchids and frankincense, in your aureole of sparkling edgeworthia dripping with the dew of the night. It is only in the night that I can see you, hovering in the blue airs of the past, mysterious and foreboding, lingering over a phrase in Tennyson you'd held your finger on in an open book you once showed me. It is during the deep hours of the grieving and incoherent night that I can remember the phrase from "Locksley Hall" that always struck me so wonderfully as a child:

> *Many a night from yonder ivied*
> *casement, ere I went to rest,*
> *Did I look on great Orion sloping*
> *slowly to the West.*
> *Many a night I saw the Pleiads,*
> *rising thro' the mellow shade,*
> *Glitter like a swarm of fire-flies*
> *tangled in a silver braid*

Osmanthus & White Pepper

When I do not see you at my bedside I am in the waking world, adrift on my own turbulent sea. The swells rise and wash over me, threaten to capsize the little boat my world floats on, and they overturn everything I've ever hoped and believed in. My books are soaked and all my beautiful clothes float like dead children scattered on the grey waves. Every time a swell comes my raisin-wrinkled fingers dig into corroded logs of sea-battered wood. The waves roll toward one another, become a larger wave, and then roll over me; in the real world my father dies of a massive leg infection, my mother falls to the ground, my dog develops heartworm, I break my ankle on the ice. I run home to crawl under the covers and it is there I find you inside my eyelids, touching with one outstretched finger a frond of gardenias to dash away a raindrop. I am adrift on the sea of misfortune and my bed is the raft; the cast iron slakes off a rusty red tide of flakes into the sea, which attracts a swarm of hungry sharks. I throw a blanket on top of me as the rain falls and when I close my eyes we're on a terrace in Nanjing made of porcelain, in the pink evening air, and we are holding hands. I am holding your hands and looking into your eyes, I am telling you I love you, that I can never stop, I am one hundred pounds lighter, that I am no longer myself; we are both wealthy and we can buy the world, we can buy love and affection, we can buy ourselves new clothing at all the H&Ms in the world, we can buy heaping plates of General Tso's chicken and potstickers and yellowed books of fortunes and histories that make no sense to us.

We cannot be together. We cannot love each other here and now. All I love is an image, a memory burned into me, a cloud of incense and white viburnum petals arranged into the form you assumed when I saw you last. You have to occupy the Eastern distances of the world entire. That is your kingdom. Your realm is the belt of Venus, the rapid cool dark that comes over us. That is your realm. You were meant to occupy it. You can only come to me here in the dark, in your purple cloud of satiny dust, your billowing raft of grief the color of a cloak in a painting by Bellini, and stare at me longingly in dark, wipe away my tears, tell me everything will work out just fine, encourage me to write as you always have, offer me a cup of tea there in the twilight of our shared memories, lovingly smile at me before you fade away. When I awake in the morning I pull my blanket over me and smile; I have seen you and the world is not all that bad, and it is while waiting for the waves to come that I can smell you on the wind, a scent of pepper and sweet peaches, your dreamtime breath hovering on the wet grey morning tide.

Sereno

The Laſh of St Francis

OR DAYS NOW, THE SEA WAS WHAT Antonio called *mar de fondo*: a groundswell that trawled up whatever was in the depths of the ocean and deposited it on the shore. A storm was on the way. The beach was littered with broken shells and dead jellies and starfish and big fat spiky purple urchins. In the morning, Ana Maria wrapped her mother's shawl around her and put on a black skirt and apron and alone, walked down the steps that led to the yellow sands, reeking with the dead flesh of the sea, the beach quivering with white birds fighting over small, mostly dead, crabs.

With a flask of fresh water mixed with rubbing alcohol Ana Maria poured a little water into the holes where the clams were, dug out the clams one by one with a gardener's spade, placed them in the basket, and continued down the beach.

She rinsed the clams in the sink at home, took a shower, luxuriated in the hot water and in the suds of the expensive Claus Porto soap she bought in Lisbon. She would not nap, because then it would be time to examine the clams, to expunge the bad ones, to leave the good ones in an ice water bath. She would then freeze them to make *cozido à portuguesa*. She hated seafood, hated *cozido à portuguesa* especially. But there was a storm on the way. And this was to be Antonio's last meal.

The storm that was to arrive, the weatherman on *Telejornal* said, was not just rainy but unusually heavy and humid, an Atlantic hurricane on the move. In the market, the coming storm had provoked discussions of all kinds. There were rumors of driftwood sighted off the coast, near Faro. The British tourists she'd met at the café downtown had all seen storms like this somewhere else: Manila, Melaka, Jakarta, Singapore. She sipped her coffee and felt a tropical breeze similar to the one that she had felt in California, in Rio de Janeiro, in Luanda where the surf sighed into the warm oblivion of a white sand beach. The wind billowed her mother's black shawl, let loose the brown hair she never could keep in place. She wanted someone in town to notice how pretty she was. No one did, and she walked back home in silence.

The house had been her grandmother's, the land on which the house sat her great-uncle's. She found Antonio in Toronto, at a conference on linguistic isolates in the Xingú river delta. They married in the second year of her PhD. She wanted to have children with him, but her cervix was too small and her eggs not viable, and she soon discovered that her doctoral program was infested with perverts and lunatics. Things might have been different had she been a little smarter, she reasoned. Now everything was a mess and it wasn't possible to live in the US anymore, because of Lucy and Mira and Camila and Jack and Cade and dozens of unnamed people, a cloud of witnesses to Antonio's insecurities, his ineptitude, his abuse.

The first victim was Lucy. Lucy was young and pretty but stupid-looking, with a small head and almond eyes and pushy lips and long black hair. She had met her at a faculty mixer one night. She wore a pale pink crop top and had a belly piercing that night and carried around a copy of *Discipline and Punish*. Ana Maria thought that Lucy was very pretentious, a baby girl of anthropology who seemed far too interested in Foucault and far too enamored with Antonio.

Antonio started coming home late from his office hours. Lucy wrote Ana Maria a terse email saying that Antonio had fingered her pussy and fucked her on his office table. Ana Maria refused to believe it, even when the ethics board chastised Antonio, and soon they were packing their bags, leaving San Francisco for San Diego, and in the Prius in the parking lot at Safeway, somewhere in Riverside, Antonio wept like a woman.

There were Mira and Camila in San Diego, pretty

Chicana studies girls that Antonio liked, girls that he sent obscene texts to. He bragged about how fat his uncut cock was, an obvious lie. Antonio never had a fat cock; he had a normal cut one like most men Ana Maria had slept with, and even if that cursory fact were true, the sex was graceless and clumsy, Antonio a fat brown turkey shaking his feathers out over her. His double chin and his nipples were repulsive.

I want to lay on top of you and cum on your beautiful brown breasts, one such text read. He'd carelessly forgot to lock his phone—he was brilliant at everything but technology—and it had been in San Diego, during one hot afternoon while she was baking a pizza in the oven and reading an ethnography about the San people that she thought it would be very nice if Antonio did not exist, should not exist at all.

The night she confronted him she stood on the pergola and swatted away the moths hovering around the string of light bulbs that hung from above.

'I want a divorce,' she said. 'Marriage counselling. Encounter weekend. Anything.'

'You're crazy, someone must have hacked my phone', he said. He laughed it off, as he always did. 'And if it were true, eh? You think I would toss away my life because of someone else? I *need* you.'

He needed her like he needed all the women in his life. His life had been one disaster after another. He needed his mother for the money he lacked for research trips. For the marriage, for the wedding banquet. The moving costs to San Francisco, borrowed from a journalist friend living in Brazil: $2000; a $300 bar tab left unpaid in Seattle during a linguistics conference, two maxed-out credit cards. He never did his laundry. She hated that he left his socks rolled up in bed—he didn't take them off like a normal man, he just rolled them off with his toes and left them to fester under the bed, and she'd have to pick them up with an attachment on the vacuum.

Ana Maria made *alcâtra* that night. He spilled beef juice on his freshly laundered blue work shirt, and the stains never came out.

'Just you wait and see, Ana Maria, it'll all come out that my phone got hacked, end of the story, nothing will happen,' he said.

'I want you to change,' she replied. 'I want you to be better than this.'

Nothing indeed happened, because by that time the IRB had suggested that he take a sabbatical to go to couples therapy, two of the girls settled with the university, and the other committed suicide. The night that Ana Maria found out one of the girls committed suicide, she caught him masturbating in the shower. She slept downstairs after that.

She looked out of the kitchen window toward the

sea. It was late afternoon. The sun was slipping behind the clouds, rendering the afternoon light diffuse. The wind was picking up. The blue shutters on the house across the street flapped in the wind and the streets were empty. The refrigerator held three potatoes, a red bell pepper, a couple of young carrots, a bunch of celery, and some chouriço. Tomorrow she would go to the butcher for ham. The clams were in a saltwater bath in a freezer in the garage.

'Could you cut that a little thicker?' she said to the butcher.

'Like this?' the butcher replied, holding up a thick slice of ham-steak.

'Like that,' she said. 'That's perfect.'

'You're pretty, way too pretty, you know that?' the young, bearded butcher said. 'Your husband must be very fortunate.'

'He forgets sometimes, but he knows it,' Ana Maria replied. 'You got a wife?'

'Yeah,' the young butcher replied. 'We've got two babies together and we couldn't be any happier.'

'Oh that's right, I met them just last week. She's very pretty, you know. She's Spanish, you said?'

'Cuban.'

'Cuban, oh well, that's something then.'

The Lash of St Francis

The young butcher with his hairy arms and his star tattoos handed her the ham without breaking the conversation.

'You've met my husband?'

'Yes,' the butcher replied. 'Interesting man. Archaeologist?'

'Anthopologist. We're both anthropologists.'

He nodded. 'What are you doing here in town? Vacation?'

'No,' she said. 'We're just visiting before my husband leaves for Africa.'

'You going with him?'

'No,' Ana Maria replied. 'I'll be heading to Brazil in a few days.'

'Oh,' the butcher replied. 'Well, since we all know one another now, you and me should get some coffee. Before the both of you leave.'

'That sounds nice,' Ana Maria replied. 'Can I think about it and get back to you? If the storm doesn't kill us all, of course.'

The butcher chuckled and shook his head. 'I'll see you at the counter, then? That'll be eight Euros.'

When she got home, she made a cup of tea and watched the *Telejornal* special report on the storm. She thought of what it would be like to run off with the butcher with the pretty Cuban wife. She imagined Antonio's car being pushed off the edge of a seaside cliff.

She wanted to be the one to do it, to steer them both off the cliff and into the sea, but she wanted to see him dying in the water, his back broken, his ribs jutting out, the car filling with water, the tide swallowing him whole.

The sea tumbled ceaselessly. It was drizzling and windy; a gray mist shrouded the headland above town. Antonio arrived in the rented grey Fiat. He shook out his coat at the door and rushed to kiss her, but she pulled away. There were fried ham-and-cheese sandwiches in a cast iron pan; she made tomato bisque and poured limeade into two glasses.

'It's getting real shitty out there,' Antonio said. 'I almost didn't make it in because the gusts were getting bad around the headlands. I saw a bunch of cork trees toppled over—'

'Tell me about it later,' Ana Maria replied.

The power went out momentarily and he sat there in the dim grey light coming through the window, the steam rising off the soup and his ham sandwich. He looked helpless. She felt sorry for him. She felt sorry that he had existed his 39 years without ever really knowing how to love someone.

After the girls, there was Cade, and Jack.

Cade had been in Antonio's sociology intro. Antonio official response to the IRB said the rubbing and grinding were accidental, but the boy reported it to the university anyway and he was moved somewhere else. No one said a thing. Antonio was writing his second book on linguistic isolates in the Xingú. The summer that he touched Cade, they went to Brazil for research. Ana Maria was doing her own book on women's work in Brazil. Then he met Jack, a graduate student.

Jack had green eyes. Nice body. Beautifully shaped eyebrows. He played soccer and the pandeiro pretty well and was a marvelous student. Antonio spent fine blue evenings with him walking on the beach in Tijuca. She knew they'd been fucking, but she said nothing. So she wrote about aggregates, wage discrimination, the inflation of the *real*, the 1964 coup d'état. When she published the book a few months later, Antonio had jettisoned Jack in Salvador da Bahia. Change in plans, Antonio said. Ana Maria wrote her soon-to-be-dead mother a letter and resolved to divorce Antonio by Christmas. Christmas came and went, and she was sitting in their house in a black funeral dress she had bought at a Nordstrom Rack in San Diego, still married to him, still unhappy, still languishing in the sun.

The complaints kept coming in. He applied for tenure in Miami. Denied. Another tenure application in Pittsburgh tabled indefinitely, because, the letters said, there were 'inconsistencies', there were 'concerns'. In February, Antonio convinced Ana Maria to move to

Portugal with him to start things new.

They were in Lisbon for three days at the Intercontinental and it was like a second honeymoon. She had forgotten what it was like to be in love with this man. They had enough money to live together like this forever, he said. But their shared credit card was declined on the first night; it had happened while they were at dinner and he was very upset with the waiter who urged him to calm down in the strictest Portuguese she had ever heard. A second credit card was tried. Also declined. She finally offered hers (the one with the good credit). An overwhelming $4,600 for two-and-a-half nights. Ana Maria slapped him in the elevator and he just stood there shaking, his eyes reddened and teary. *I do these things because I love you*, he said, *I do it because after all we've been through you're the only one who still loves me*, and when they got back to the hotel room he sloppily fucked her in the shower and promised to see a priest. The next day they drove to the Algarve, bills paid. He said he was receiving some money from a wire from some distant relatives in Amherst. The wire came that morning and miraculously it wasn't fraudulent.

The rain let up for a half-hour and they took a walk down to the cliffside. A huge sneaker wave had caught a group of British surfers off-guard. The wave roared ashore and crashed against the side of the cliff, and Ana Maria and Antonio felt the earth tremble under them. The surfers had been swept up in the wave, but she couldn't see where the wave had taken them.

'Idiots, all of them,' he said.

'You don't know that,' Ana Maria responded. 'Don't judge them because you can't do what they're doing.'

'I wanted to.'

'But you can't now, can you,' Ana Maria replied.

'They're dead, I just know it,' he said.

'Oh my god, Antonio, just *shut up*. 'You're overthinking this. They probably just got washed into a corner we couldn't see.'

'You know how small that inlet is,' he replied. 'The water could have pushed them against the rocks.'

'And they still would have survived.'

They walked back home. They had considerable trouble ascending the hill back to the house and struggled against the onslaught of the wind. Branches began falling from the trees. The power lines whistled. The electricity flickered. Then came the first bands of heavy rain, which lasted for hours.

The transformer across the street finally exploded around 8 p.m. and the power cut out for good.

He built a fire in the living room and they ate what was left of the soup.

'Once all of this is done,' he said quietly, 'we really should start thinking about what we want the rest of our lives to look like.'

'I like this town. I like the people... they all seem very nice. I talked to the butcher today, when I was getting the alheira; he seemed very friendly.'

'The guy with the star tattoos on his fingers?'

'Yeah, him. How'd you know about him?

'The same guy who was walking his dog the other night in town. A young guy, maybe twenty-five, twenty-six. Yeah, he was very nice. Beautiful wife.'

'So I hear.'

She watched him stare into the fire.

'I could have been that guy. We could have had it all figured out, Ana Maria. Imagine.' He took a ragged breath and drank his whiskey. 'That could have been us.'

She stared back into the fire with him and said nothing.

Around 2 a.m., a tree crashed somewhere, and the house rattled. Ana Maria got up and looked out the dark window in the kitchen. The street was blanketed with broken branches and debris. She came back into the bedroom and he was on his phone, the eerie blue glow of his phone illuminating his chubby brown face in the dark.

'I think the big broom tree in the street just fell over,' Ana Maria said.

'That sucks,' he said, not taking his gaze off his phone. 'I'm barely getting any signal at all. I just checked the weather and it took forever to load.'

'Let's just go back to sleep, honey.'

She crawled back into bed and pulled the covers over herself. He turned over on his side. The phone's screen cast a false dawn over the horizon of his naked body, so that she could see the hair on his arms and shoulders.

As she was drifting back to sleep, he let out a deep, embarrassing fart in bed. The smell was awful. Ana Maria wanted to get up, kill him right then and there, but it was cold and she was tired. She sighed and put her pillow over her face and breathed in.

'I'm sorry,' he said, before he put away the phone. He yawned loudly. Even farting and yawning for him came with an air of self-congratulation. The room was dark and smelled of rotten eggs and sweaty ass. Ana Maria stared at the crucifix on the wall on her side of the room, dimly illuminated.

Ana Maria showered in the morning. There was enough hot water for just one shower. She put on a little perfume, and put on an oversized green sweater and a pair of blue jeans and some white tennis shoes. The power was back on and everything that had a digital clock blinked 12:00 as if to tell Ana Maria that zero hour had come.

She made coffee. She cracked two eggs in a pan and fried up some ham steaks. She pulled out a glass pitcher and filled it with orange juice concentrate.

She went to her purse and pulled out a small bottle of eye drops. She went back to the kitchen and poured herself a glass of juice. She drank the glass of orange juice. She pulled out the bottle of eye drops and squeezed half of it into the pitcher, stirred it, and reserved it in the refrigerator.

He came out for breakfast clad only in a dingy white towel wrapped around his waist.

'Breakfast is ready, serve yourself,' she said.

'I guess the power's back on?'

'Yeah. Get dressed and come and eat breakfast with me.'

He disappeared back into the bedroom and came out in a t-shirt and jeans and his dingy tennis shoes.

'Did you find out whose tree fell?'

'Senhora Joana's, across the street. It was her broom tree.'

'That's a shame,' he said.

'There's juice in the fridge if you want it,' she replied.

She watched as he poured himself a large glass of juice and chugged about half of it. He sat down and smiled. He looked out of the window for a long time.

'First time you've made this for me in a while.'

'I felt like being nice today,' she replied.

'How is that different from any other day? You're always nice to me.'

'Today is different,' Ana Maria replied. 'Today is special.'

She determined what she would say if and when the police were to show up. She reasoned that if he were to survive and went to the police, she'd kill herself by walking into the sea like her grandmother had. There could be no life or freedom if Antonio kept on living; eight drops of Visine could kill a small dog, ten a small child, twelve an adult man. Eight for her if the police had her cornered, or if something were to go wrong. Ten if the shit really hit the fan.

I had no idea about the eye drops. Yes, he had an infection in his eyes. He had problems with his eyes. No, we didn't argue.

She defrosted the clams after breakfast. She sauteed the onion, the celery, the potatoes, the bell pepper. She fried the last ham steak and the chouriço. She pulled out her grandmother's large stock pot and covered the clams with water. She boiled the clams until they opened, drained them, and then poured in everything else into the dry stock pot. She cut up a fennel bulb, parsley, and got the Piri-Piri out of the refrigerator. He always ate his cozido with Piri-Piri. She boiled the soup, uncorked a bottle of vinho verde, poured herself a glass, had another, looked at her phone. The entire process of putting the soup together, she surmised, took little more than four hours.

He came in once more to have another glass of orange juice. He drank the entire glass right there in front of her. He said he was thirsty, he said he was writing some emails; they'd be returning to Lisbon next Monday to meet with another publisher. He pissed in the bathroom, he washed his hands, he kissed her and said she was beautiful. She poured herself a glass of water, sat down at the kitchen table and wrote a letter to no one, tore that letter up, wrote a letter to her best friend in California instead.

Catherine, this is to tell you

'Look honey, I see some sunlight peeking through the clouds outside,' he said, looking out on the blasted countryside, the rain-stained black rocks, the grey surf. 'We should take a walk later.'

Catherine this is to tell you that Antonio is dead. He died suddenly on 4 October. I don't know what to tell you because I'm still in shock. Catherine, my husband and my friend is gone and I don't know what I am going to do

Catherine this is to let you know that
Antonio died this afternoon
~~Antonio isn't alive~~
~~Antonio passed away suddenly~~

The Lash of St Francis

<s>*Myocardial infarction*</s>
Heart attack
Suicide, they're saying
<s>*I had no idea*</s> *he was depressed*

The sun was pouring through the kitchen window when he got home. He hung his coat up on the wall and took his shoes off in the foyer. He asked when dinner was. She said 6 p.m.

'Those guys we saw yesterday are alive,' he said. 'Just fine.'

'Oh really?'

'Yeah. They offered me a cup of coffee, but I wanted to get home for the *cozido*. I thought we could have coffee later, just you and me.'

When six came, she deleted her search terms on her phone.

Ana Maria knew the sunlight was false: it was just the eye of the storm passing over. She opened up another bottle of *vinho verde*, the $40 bottle she bought from a man in Lisbon just for this occasion, put that bottle on ice. She pulled down a white sheet and laid it on the dining room table, set the table, placed two large white bowls on the table. She spooned the *cozido* into a tureen and covered it. She went into the bathroom, peed, knocked back a glass of water, and then returned to the dining room table. She poured herself another tall glass of vinho verde. She took out the bottle of eye drops and squeezed it all out into the bottle of wine. She went back to the bathroom and flushed the empty bottle of eyedrops down the toilet.

'I was reading something interesting… about the storm,' he said that evening at dinner.

'What's that?' Ana Maria said.

'An interesting bit of weather lore. Very strong storms usually show up around this time, late September and early October.'

'Like hurricanes?'

'Sometimes like hurricanes, yes. You know, my scholar friend, Dr Corrêia—he said once people used to call this storm "the lash of St Francis" because storms like this happened to fall on his feast day. It's October 4th, isn't it?'

'It's October third,' Ana Maria replied.

He closed his eyes and mulled over the words he had just pronounced, as if he were reciting some enchantment. 'The *lash* of St Francis. I have to admit, it's a very pretty term, a little high-flown, maybe… the idea of St Francis punishing the world with the cord on his habit… as if we needed to be punished.'

He sipped his wine again and smiled at her. She said nothing.

'It's good wine, you know,' he said, with a slight

chuckle. Forty dollars, you said? Not too bad for half-decent *vinho verde*.'

'Well then,' she said, raising her glass. 'Here's to us.'

Sereno

The Hunter

AT 28, NATE HAD REACHED A POINT WHERE his lat spread WAS at fifty-five inches, his biceps were peaked cold at twenty-one inches, and he had a low resting heart rate. Monday nights were all about back and chest, seated rows. He was told to never force the rep. To Nate, though, the rep was meant to be completed to force, just as breathing for him was full of intention.

Nate lived off of unemployment and an occasional training gig. His life was building up a body, soaking it in ice water and steaming it in a bath, having the massage therapist rub it out in the dim grey room in the house she lived in. He ate brown rice and soy curls in sock feet and watched Netflix. Sometimes he played a video game. He slept dreamlessly. He had no girlfriend, had never bothered to think of women. He ate, slept, showered like a bodybuilder. He lived at the very end of a headland, in a small house among a copse of Douglas firs. He drove a Jeep and did not concern himself much with the world outside of Metlako.

To make ends meet, he'd train traveling businessmen, soccer moms, whiny fat people, salty old grandmas who usually did as they were told. He'd sit in the office in the November dark watching the rain slough off the plate-glass window of the gym. Then the gym would close and Nate would walk back home, strip to his briefs, fall asleep on the low futon his mother found for him at Walmart.

In the morning the grey light revealed a sad landscape of sweaty yesterdays, piles of rank gym clothes and pissy-smelling jockstraps. He would pick it all up, throw it into a hamper, do the laundry, and scroll through Instagram.

On the morning of his twenty-ninth birthday, Tanner showered and shaved and waited for Ricky to call. He did not even know Ricky's last name; they'd shared a few drinks at the club and some dirty dances and a bump of coke and eventually the mattress on the floor of Tanner's condo. Ricky made Tanner horny and nervous. So he walked to the Mall behind the condo complex, bought an ice cream cone, and waited for Ricky's FaceTime call.

'Forget about him. You can start over again,' Ricky told him over the phone. Tanner aimlessly drifted from storefront to storefront at the Mall, ambulating from a Yankee Candle to a Spencer's full of middle school kids.

'Fuck George. He couldn't love you the way you needed to be loved.'

Tanner let out an exasperated sigh. This was not how he had wanted to spend Sunday afternoon. 'I don't want to talk about George anymore.'

'Do you know what you need?' Ricky said. 'You need a long vacation. You could pull some money together and we could go to Palm Springs.'

'I don't have that type of money,' Tanner said.

'Didn't George leave you anything?'

'No. He took everything. You saw my apartment. All I've got is the food in the fridge. My clothes. The bills.'

'But you know someone that can get you the money somehow, right?' Ricky said. 'You're a banker, right?'

'I'm a teller. Not a banker.'

'But you can get the money, right?,' Ricky replied. Tanner stared ahead at the Puffle Waffle lady pouring sticky batter into a machine and pressing it closed. He smelled the sugar burn in the stale air of the mall.

'Hello? Can you hear me?'

'When do you think you can host me?' Tanner said.

'I don't know. If you get some money, you can come over this weekend. No one is here. And I miss you. You know I miss you.'

Tanner walked back home with the cigarette

dangling in his mouth, thinking of Ricky's body, the short stubble on his chin. Two days. Two days to get the money transferred from one account to another, without raising hell. It'd take fifteen minutes to get the application signed, a few minues to get an ATM card. Two days, fifteen minutes. Compliance wouldn't know or care, because he could just resign if it looked bad. He could take the money and run. Ricky would be there in San Diego waiting for him by the poolside in a pair of Andrew Christians, cocktail in hand. It could be that easy.

'And how are *you* this morning?' the old man said, hobbling into Tanner's bank with his oiled bamboo cane. This old man smelled of Old Spice and brilliantine, and wore Hawaiian shirts, even when it was cold. He called himself Walter, but Tanner knew his legal name was Geoffrey David Higgins.

'Walter,' Tanner replied, with a note of weariness in his voice.

'Tell me,' Walter said, putting his cane down on the teller's desk. 'Those Russian sunflowers I gave you. Did you give them a good home?'

'They're on my windowsill at home.'

Walter gasped with delight. 'Oh, that sounds *darling*. You're *so* sweet.'

The Hunter

'Of course,' Tanner replied. He cleared his throat. 'What can I help you out with today?'

Walter smiled. 'The usual. Just depositing into the money market account I have. Did you know I'm planning to travel to Provence soon? With another gentleman friend.'

'Provence,' Tanner replied, feigning interest.

He had memorized the account number. He took note of the balances. He carefully clicked his mouse. The time was 12:39 PM.

'Have you been working out lately?' Walter asked. 'Your shoulders look really pumped up.'

'Oh,' Tanner said. 'Not really. I just like to dance.'

Walter looked at Tanner's coworker. She'd been carefully watching Tanner's terminal.

'That color suits you just fine,' Walter said to the coworker. 'Teal is *just* your color.'

'You OK?' the coworker said.

'Yeah, I'm fine,' Tanner said, not looking up. 'So it looks like we're gonna have to service your account; for

what reason I don't know. Money market account looks like it's all good though. I'll print you a receipt.'

'I'm sure you'll get it all squared away,' Walter said. 'What are you doing this evening?'

'I'm going home and drinking a big stout,' Tanner replied.

Walter passed a crisp white envelope under the Plexiglass window to Tanner.

'I've got a pretty good stock of German stouts if you want to try some.'

Tanner deposited the check into Walter's checking account. All in all, it took just ten, ten-and-a-half minutes. The system had locked him out twice. On the third try, the money was transferred to another account he had access to. Walter stood there like a daft, fat, clueless penguin.

'When I come back, I'm bringing you some potted lavender. Didn't you say that George liked lavender?'

'George doesn't live with me anymore,' Tanner said. 'Moved out a month ago.'

'Ah, I'm so sorry; I didn't know. Well, in any case. Lavender for you, then.'

The Hunter

He handed Walter the receipt. After it was all done he heaved a sigh and took a long drink of water from his water bottle. His coworker crossed her arms, then turned on her heel and walked out of the break room.

'Stupid bitch,' he said under his breath.

When five o'clock came the system raised two red flags. Tanner's manager went to his terminal.

'Oh, it's *this* error again,' she said. 'Jeannie had this happen last month. You moved money from Walter's money market account?'

'Uh, I did... I got a message that account needed servicing.'

The manager pushed her glasses up the bridge of her nose and clicked around the window.

'I'm sure you'll be OK. He deposited $70,000 today. His check, right? That was what the check was for?'

'Yes,' Tanner said. 'Yes, that's what it was.'

'No worries, then. Everything checks out,' the manager said. 'Gosh, I hate this system that we're using.'

Tanner felt a wave of panic wash over him and recede, fading away into a flush of pins and needles in his feet. The manager typed an override code into the terminal.

'Next time, just tell me when he's depositing large amounts and I'll do this for you. I'd really like it if you didn't flirt with Walter so much, by the way.'

'He flirts with *me*.'

'Potted lavender? Are you *kidding* me?.'

After the tills were counted, Tanner had his manager cash him out. He needed precisely $3000. She slowly and carefully counted out $2,500 in $10 bills on the table. Tanner watched her count out the money as if he were watching a baby being born.

'Two-thousand-four-hundred and ninety, twenty-five hundred. Are you paying off a student loan, or what?'

'First and last month of a new apartment.'

'What a *prick* George is,' the manager said, putting the money in a brown zip pouch. 'My kid might be interested in making a little extra cash moving furniture if you need a hand.'

The Hunter

He tossed the pouch into the passenger seat of his car and buried his face into the steering wheel. The weak sun warmed the leatherette of the steering wheel. He clenched his eyes shut, wondering what to do next. After ten minutes of heavy breathing, he turned on the car and pulled out of the parking lot.

He went home, stripped off his clothing, took a hot shower, ate out of a can of Beefaroni, then put on a tank and some running shorts. He drove out of Roseland. He kept on driving east until he was close to Mount Manresa, then pulled off the side of the road to a tackle shop abutting a woody creek.

At the tackle shop he bought some beef jerky, smoked a cigarette, and scrolled some posts on Facebook to clear his head. He went back into the store to use the ATM ten minutes later. He pulled out $500, the maximum amount for withdrawals at that ATM. He stuffed the brown pouch into the glovebox.

He drove back home. He pulled all clothes off the hangers and threw them into the trunk of his SUV. He pulled out his blue suede Gucci pumps, his Dockers loafers, his Vineyard Vines, his ratty Payless topsiders, the flip flops he had bought once on vacation in Hawaii, his serpentine piles of neckties, his stinking mountain of colognes and salves. Everything smelled of cigarettes, of the gay bar, of his ex-boyfriend, of his ex-boyfriend's nasty cologne. He tore off the bedsheets and the comforter, piled all of that into the SUV, went to the kitchen, gathered an armful of Chef Boyardee, and put everything not perishable in a cardboard box that was on the verge of collapse.

He put on a hoodie and started the car. It was drizzling. He accelerated out of the condo gate and tossed the house keys into the illuminated fountain at the entrance. *Everything will be OK now*, he thought. *This is where I get to be me again.*

He took the scenic highway out to the coast, anticipating that someone would assume he'd take I-205 to San Francisco with the money. To clear his mind, he turned on Spotify, sang a few Rihanna songs out loud, rolled down the window to smoke and smell the rain-soaked air. Gradually the lights and traffic winnowed to a single thread of fuzzy light stitching itself into the dark of the Coast Range forest.

After passing through the mist, the SUV descended a mountain pass. The coastline was visible, the dark hem of the earth shrouded in mist. The air was distinctly colder when he stopped into the gas station to refill.

The Hunter

'Marlboro Reds,' Tanner said to the gas station attendant.

'Sure thing,' the gas station attendant said, reaching under the counter for a pack.

'Where am I?'

'Metlako, Oregon,' the attendant said.

'How far is it to leave the state entirely?'

'About four hours,' the attendant replied.

Tanner reached into his wallet and slid a crisp $50 bill across the counter.

'You know any good places to eat around here?'

'No,' the attendant replied, taking the $50 bill.

That afternoon, Nate ate a yam and a chicken breast at the gym and went for a long walk up to Fine Point. A buck emerged from the Sitka spruces and stared at him. The buck was big and muscular like Nate, a real ten-point buck that looked like an alpha. A large truck slowed to a halt in front of the buck. The buck bowed its head, pawed at the ground, moved off to the side of the highway, and leapt into the green wet meadow. Nate looked at the truck driver.

The truck driver waved to him. The sun came out from behind a cloud.

'But you'll be in San Francisco in about six hours, right?' Ricky said.

'I have to think. I don't know if I'll have time to sleep and eat before I leave Oregon.'

'You sound like a train wreck,' Ricky said.

There was some static on the phone line.

'I'm fine, it's just a storm passing through,' Tanner replied. He looked out at the angry sea, the clouds turning blue and grey in the fading light of the day. 'I've got some Valium, I should be fine.'

'Go buy a Rockstar and start thinking about how you want to get down here,' Ricky replied. 'And call me tonight, please?'

There was a Grindr notification on Nate's phone. The *frrup* interrupted the quiet of his darkened room. The

message was brief, obscene. The same man as the night before, a fifty-seven-year-old rancher in Sanpoil, but no pictures of his junk this time.

'Let me put my tongue up your tight asshole,' the message read.

That man. Ugly. Old face. Wrinkled turkey neck.

No. He hit the block button, got up, took a shower, and decided on a walk into town to get some dinner.

With the sky already fading to a deep blue, Tanner pulled off the road into a secluded beach to plan the rest of the trip to San Francisco.

It had rained all day. A few errant birds on the beach. The sea looked confused, glassy-eyed, turbulent. Tanner smoked a cigarette and walked along the county access road to the beach. Happy people everywhere— wide-eyed boys, old men in RVs with baseball caps that read IT'S BEER O'CLOCK, women with oily Tupperware full of tuna sandwiches, boys building a bonfire with driftwood and sappy kindling. Tanner thought of Ricky, Ricky's body, the parties in WeHo and Palm Springs Ricky had bragged about. He thought of a piano-shaped pool in a magazine article. He thought of Frank Sinatra.

Sereno

'There's my favorite muscleman,' Darlene said.

'*Stahhhp*,' Nate said, smiling. 'I'm here for the usual.'

'Francisco,' Darlene called to the cook in the diner kitchen. '*Un* cheeseburger, *por favor*.'

Nate took off his cap and set it on the counter. Darlene smiled at him.

'When are you going to come up to the house and visit me?' Darlene said, pouring him some very dark coffee in a very white ceramic mug. 'Better yet, when are you going to visit Allison for dinner?'

Nate smiled. 'She's nice. I *do* like her. It *has* been a while.'

'But?' Darlene said. 'Let me guess: she's not your type.'

'I never said that,' Nate replied. 'I didn't say that *at all*.'

'You can't live the way you do,' Darlene replied gently, like the mother she was. 'No parents, no relatives out here. You can't just live in a gym all by yourself. You gotta *socialize*, honey.'

The Hunter

Tanner checked Scruff and there was Nate, looking intimidating, flexing at the camera, in a skimpy neon orange tank top. Nate was not Nate, though: the profile simply read HUNTER, 28, body type muscular, no indication if he was a top or bottom, or even if he was real.

'He's a catfish,' Tanner said to himself in the snack aisle of the grocery store. 'This motherfucker is a catfish, I just know it.'

He hesitated, wondering if he should write anything at all.

Finally, he typed: 'Are you real?'

Nate walked home. The night was a bust. Nate was a midnight man in a ten o'clock town. Darlene had no way of knowing what Nate really wanted. And he couldn't verbalize it, even if he wanted to.

No one could know, unless they wanted to.

He showered, moisturized his skin, rubbed analgesic into his sore right tricep.

He stood at the foot of the bed in his underwear, contemplating responding to Tanner, just to see if he'd be interested in talking rather than fucking. He looked like what everyone else who wanted sex from Nate looked like—had wanted what everyone else wanted—to fuck, not to talk.

The guys were usually married, bored and lonely, or just passing through.

Tanner looked goofy. There was something artificial to him. His dated haircut. A very obvious professional headshot. His shirtless photos showed someone with great pecs. *Maybe*, Nate thought to himself, *maybe he might be a good gym buddy.*

'Yeah I'm real,' he typed back. He waited a few minutes for the man to respond, the chat bubble wavering, inflating, deflating.

Tanner responded: 'Are you doing anything tonight? I'm spending the weekend in town.'

Tanner met Nate at the end of Clarke Street. It was 8:30. Everything was closed. The cold, wet wind blew through the telephone wires.

'Your biceps are huge. They're bigger than my head,' Tanner said.

The Hunter

'Thanks, I guess,' Nate said.

'You live here? You work here?'

'In the gym, across the street,' Nate replied. 'I live at the end of the inlet.'

'You wanna train me? I could use a workout or two.'

'Depends on how long you're gonna be here.'

'Until my boss tells me it's OK to leave. I'm here on business,' Tanner replied. 'You're a lot bigger in person than in your picture, you know that?'

Nate smiled, said nothing, shrugged it off.

Of course he would say that. *Of course.*

The gym was empty when Tanner and Nate arrived. Someone had left the radio on. The rain was falling in sheets against the window, leaking through the cracks in fat drops that spattered the blue workout mat Tanner and Nate stood on.

Tanner felt Nate's hands on his waist as he clenched the bar. He lowered his body and Nate lowered his with him. The bar was cold, felt heavy. Tanner's back muscles flushed with pain as he completed the squat. It was only fifty pounds but it still hurt like hell. The music was aggressive, loud, artificial.

'You got this?' Nate said. 'Don't stop, go all the way down and come back all the way up. Do another one.'

'OK,' Tanner replied, exhaling nervously. 'It's just that I'm soft, is all.'

'You got this, Tanner. Do another.'

He did another squat and pushed his back out, brushed against Nate's thighs.

'Oh, I'm sorry,' Nate said, moving back a little.

Tanner put the bar back on its rest and turned to face Nate. Nate looked embarrassed, a little bored. Tanner stepped closer until he was against Nate's big body. Tanner ran his hand up Nate's shredder tank.

There were those green eyes again. Nate's felt his heart throb once, twice. Sweat gathered in his palms.
'You wanna take a shower?' Tanner asked.

They went to the back of the gym. Nate locked the door to the bathroom; they were momentarily entombed in the damp, cool dark. He flipped on the light over the bathroom sink. In the dim light, he stripped Tanner, wrapped himself in Tanner's arms, put his tongue inside his mouth. Tanner had once fucked a guy in a shower in a bathhouse in Roseland; an old man, but he had never been with someone who had initiated the sex before. They took turns fucking each other in the shower. Tanner's body felt locked into Nate's; they fit perfectly within one another. After they finished they stood under the showerhead and let the hot water cascade over them. Nate put his head on Tanner's shoulder and closed his eyes.

They piled into Tanner's SUV afterward and for a few minutes they both stared at their phones, trying to find a place that served pancakes at 2 a.m. Tanner drove them to a Pig & Pancake in Newport. The pancake house was immense, loud, and crowded at 3 a.m. There were rowdy crowds of college kids from Roseland, wide-eyed tourists, exhausted-looking parents with rambunctious, sleepless four year olds.

'You want me to get the bill?' Nate said.

'No,' Tanner replied. 'I'll be right back, though.'

He went to the bathroom just as breakfast was being brought to the table and counted out the $3,000 in a stall once, twice, three times, four times. He was worried someone would notice him. Worried even more if cops showed up.

Back at the table, he downed half a tab of Valium with orange juice. Nate looked beautiful under the light above the booth. *It's gonna be OK. I can try to relax with this guy*, Tanner thought.

'Dad was a game hunter,' Nate said to Tanner that night in bed.

'What did he hunt?'

'Deer, primarily. Sometimes elk. We had a lot of venison jerky in the house growing up. He taught me how to hunt and fish. I usually bow hunt this time of year.'

'And your mom?'

'She lives in California,' Nate replied. 'She didn't like the hunting too much, I guess. Dad was gone almost all the time.'

'A survivalist,' Tanner replied. 'With crossbows. How medieval.'

'Yeah, that's me and Dad for sure,' Nate replied,

chuckling. 'Always scraping by somehow. You ever hunt or fish?'

'No. My family is as urban as they come. All from Keizer. I think my Uncle Ted shot a bear in the seventies, though.'

'Really?'

'Oh yeah, he brings out the story every Thanksgiving. Every year it gets more ridiculous.'

Nate chuckled, looked at Tanner, exhaled, luxuriated in this silence between them. Tanner planted a kiss inbetween Nate's pecs.

'I've never ever dated a guy before,' Nate said.

'You're not gay?'

'No, I'm gay; no one knows.'

Tanner stared at the ceiling and let Nate's confession hang in the air.

'I've learned to look after myself,' Nate said. "I don't give a fuck if anyone knows about me liking dudes. I figure most people think I am, with the way I work out.'

'I would have never guessed,' Tanner replied. 'I

don't think people here would mind, though. Everyone here seems nice.'

'They're nice to people from *Roseland*,' Nate finished. 'That's the difference. Usually people from Roseland aren't nice to people from Metlako. Not everyone. But you're pretty nice.'

'*Pretty* nice?'

'Well, you get me though, right?' Nate replied. 'Like, you're not an asshole. At least I don't think you could be.'

'No,' Tanner replied. 'No, I don't think I could be, not to you at least, I think.' He sighed. 'To be honest with you, I don't know what you see in me.'

'You have pretty eyes,' Nate then said, squeezing Tanner's hand.

'When are you going to be down here?' Ricky said over the phone the next morning.

'I don't know. Maybe tonight? Something happened. Something I wasn't expecting.'

'What happened,' Ricky replied.

The Hunter

The sun was passing between the clouds. There was a silvery glint on the sea. Tanner was in the driver seat of the SUV, watching Nate fish his phone out of his pocket at the scenic overlook. He gestured to Tanner to come out of the car and look at the tide coming in.

'Just something I wasn't expecting. A minor setback. I'll tell you about it later tonight.'

'Don't pull out on me, Tanner,' Ricky replied, with a threat in his tone. 'Dont do this to me. I hope you're not having second thoughts.'

'I'm not,' Tanner replied, watching Nate take a selfie. Nate beckoned him out of the car.

'Listen, let me call you later,' Tanner said.

'Hold me closer! Don't stop hugging me,' Tanner said. He could feel Nate's biceps constrict his chest. The feeling was sensational. They were on Otter Creek Rock, with about a dozen other folks pulled over on the side of the road, embracing each other in the face of the cold gale that came off the sea. He could smell the salt of the morning surf in his nostrils.

'You didn't tell me how cold it gets here. I can't feel my fingers. We should have just stayed home.'

Sereno

'But you said you wanted to see Otter Creek Rock. You wanna go back home and get warmed up?'

Tanner tugged on Nate's hoodie and kissed him deeply. The rain spattered his face; he could smell Nate's cologne. The escape out of Oregon had been compromised. It was too hard to let go now. Of course he wanted to build a fire with Nate. Of course he wanted to go back home. Of course he wanted to see him naked again, to feel his heavy pecs in his hands, to kiss him; to never, ever stop kissing him.

Nate cut up a kabocha squash and put it in the oven. He sautéed some chicken breast, an onion, made some quinoa, uncorked a cheap Malbec and poured it into two mason jars. He handed one mason jar to Tanner, who was sitting on the couch in his underwear. Tanner felt like he was seventeen again, as if he were sleeping over at the house of a boy he was forbidden to speak to.

'I'm not planning to stay here,' Tanner said. 'But I'm having second thoughts.'

'Second thoughts, really?'

'Yeah,' he said, sipping the wine. 'I should get going…I have business in San Francisco.'

The Hunter

'Think about staying with me a few more days. I could drive you around. Show you a few more places. I could take you hunting.'

'Hunting?'

'You've never been? We have to go. I've got a crossbow you could learn with too.' Nate put his big hands on Tanner's shoulders and squeezed them. 'Tanner. Listen to me. Whatever you want to do, we'll do.'

Tanner went outside for a smoke and stared into the grey-green water that abutted the rocky tongue of land that Nate's house sat on. The afternoon was stern, dismal, damp, fading to a sad bluish-grey. Patches of blue sky were opening up in the clouds.

Nate was his. He had to get rid of the money somehow. Drop it off, claim it was a mistake, face the consequences, alter them, obliterate the money, toss the money from Otter Creek Rock, or Fine Point, or *somewhere*, let the money fly away into the wind, let someone else find it, leave it in the parking lot at some credit union in Metlako, burn it in the wood stove in Nate's place, spend it on a new car for Nate, let Nate use the money to build up his body even more and fix up the house he lived in, let him have the money to redecorate, to buy white sheer curtains for the bare window with the

Venetian blinds above Nate's futon. Or he could buy Nate a real bed, a new wardrobe, an eventual trip to Hawaii, a night in an anonymous hotel room in Kawaii, far from all this November rain, in some halcyon place where all the mistakes Tanner had made could be simply willed away, forgotten, consigned to a warm turquoise sea.

It could be as easy as just making a phone call, he told himself. It would be OK because Nate would be waiting for him after it all ended, in whichever way it would end. He would wait for him. Nate could make space for him in that little house and it would be completely OK.

Nate lay on his futon, looking dreamily as Tanner mounted him. Tanner let Nate run his calloused hands over his chest, his stomach, down under his thighs. Tanner stared into Nate's eyes. He let him have what he wanted. Tanner felt enervated, grateful, alive, secure in himself at last. He let Nate roll over on him, let him lift his legs high in the air, let him conquer and possess Tanner's body, let him plunder it with his mouth and his hands. Together they became a strange, wondrous creature made of muscle, skin, and sweat. The sunset came through the window like shaft of gold filled with motes of sparkling dust, and the warmth of the light filled Nate and Tanner's bodies like a pitcher filling with water, until Nate could not hold back anymore. He came on Tanner's back. He breathlessly rolled over onto his side and let out a giddy chuckle. Tanner put his arms around Nate's immense body and kissed his sweaty brow. Nate felt Tanner's hot, flushed cheek, the trickle of jism in the gutter of his abs, the flutter of his eyelash, the scruff of an unshaved cheek.

Nate hopped in the shower afterward and Tanner went out. He walked down to the SUV and opened a fresh pack of cigarettes. The brown zip bag lay there in the passenger seat, burning a hole into the wine-dark sea of Tanner's mind. Every time he would think of being with Nate, the thought of the money would swell and glow like the cherry of his cigarette, obliterating everything good that Tanner felt within him. He had another cigarette, did not once take his gaze off of the sight of the zip bag, laying there malevolently in the passenger seat like a child that could not be left alone. Tanner flicked away the cigarette into the pine straw, grabbed the pouch, and walked back into the house.

He lay back in the futon and turned on the TV. There were already plans for a full day: he'd go to the grocery store, make a casserole for Nate, get coffee at the Dutch Bros in Metlako, neither worrying nor caring what people might say. He would kiss him. And then he would stay. He would return the money, forget about Ricky, do the right thing. The money was a non-issue. It was time to start all over again.

He mindlessly channel-surfed for a few minutes

before settling on the 11 o'clock news out of Roseland. He shot straight up in bed when he saw his own face staring back at him from the TV screen. The chyron on screen read WANTED FOR FRAUD. The state police had put out an APB for him. The make and the model of the SUV were onscreen, along with his awful driver's license photo, and the untrue assertion that he was to be considered armed and dangerous. His heart thundered inside him. His chest tightened. The world was closing in on him. He felt like the earth was opening itself up to swallow him whole.

'I don't want you to leave,' Nate said that night. The moonlight passed through the blinds and onto his chest. 'Stay with me. Please.'

Tanner felt a terrible sadness come over him as Nate moved in close to cuddle him.

'You don't have to worry about finding a new job, at least not for a while. I could take care of us,' Nate went on. 'I could cook for us... take us hunting...we could rent a cabin up in the mountains. I have a friend of mine who owns one.'

'It would be nice,' Tanner replied, emotionless.

'Think about it,' Nate replied, peppering Tanner's

shoulder with kisses. 'What we got we don't have to let no one else know about.'

Nate let out a gratified sigh and rubbed his stubble into Tanner's shoulder and cheek. 'I'm glad I found you.'

'Let's try to get some sleep,' Tanner replied.

At around 4 a.m., when Nate had finally loosened his hands around Tanner's waist, Tanner got up, put on his clothes, grabbed his bag, and quietly left the house. He didn't bother looking back: he walked to the end of the drive,and got into the SUV.

His hands clenched the steering wheel. He hesitated, staring back at the solitary light on in Nate's house. He heaved a frustrated, angry sigh. He turned on the SUV and sped off down the road and out of town.

The next day, Nate found a brown zip bag with $3,000 in $20 bills on the kitchen counter, with a hastily written note from a yellow legal pad advising Nate to call the cops. Nate sat on the stool in the kitchen and read the note over and over, counted the money, took it out, inspected it, smelled it, and put the money away. He called the cops and calmly told the dispatcher what had happened. Nate put on his blue jeans and walked outside, just as the rain began descending like a white veil over the pines.

'And you're sure he didn't take anything,' the chubby state police officer said.

'No,' Nate replied, quietly.

'I'm sorry for pointing my weapon at you like I did earlier,' the state police officer said. 'Guys like him you can't mess around with.'

The officer took one last glance at Nate's messy house.

'He didn't say where he was heading to?'

'No.'

Nate sat on the wooden steps of his little house and buried his face in his hands.

'You an athlete or a personal trainer or something?'

'Yeah,' Nate replied, trying not to break out in a sob. The tears were coming hard and fast; he wasn't sure if he could keep his composure.

'Well, I guess if he didn't take anything I should be on my way,' the officer said. He handed Nate his card. 'Give me a call if I there's anything else I can help out with. Or if he comes back.'

Nate kept one hand over his eyes, and quickly pocketed the card.

'You have a good day, now,' the officer said.

Nate sat, his eyes tightly shut, listening to the police officer's footsteps fade. He heard the officer open his car door and utter something unintelligible over the radio. The police car backed out of the drive and onto the highway. He heard the the rain, the blackbirds in the pines, and the rough sea. Nate had the silence again.

After Nate finished sobbing in the shower, he put on his clothes and running shoes and walked along the highway and on toward town to work out. The mist had broken up and the sun was resplendent over the inlet. The sound of the sea beneath the cliffs murmered gently. Nate walked down the hill, away from the headland, down the curve that led into town. The asphalt sparkled with fresh rain.

At the end of the curve, in a culvert, Nate found the carcass of the buck he'd seen on the highway. His heart sank. He walked up to the dead animal, laying in the brilliant afternoon sun. The buck's eyes were wide open. Its snout swarmed with flies; its mouth was full of maggots. Its crown was massive, covered in velvet and spattered with blood. He knew it had suffered greatly before it died. The coyotes were on their way. Even in death, the buck was the most beautiful thing

Nate had ever seen.

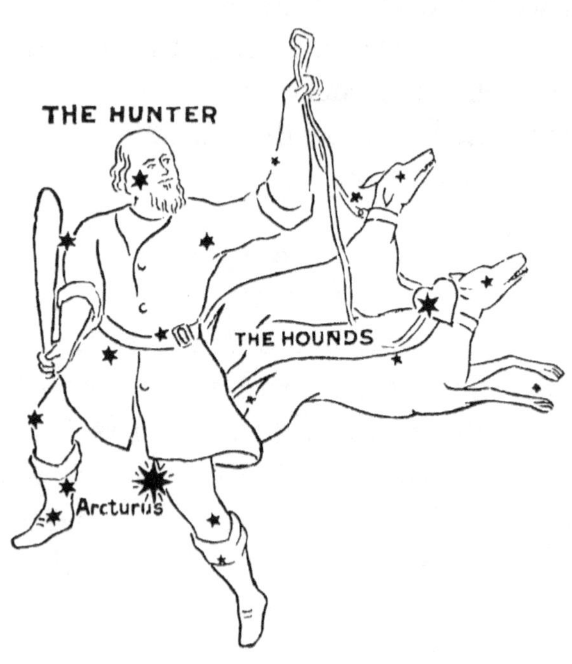

The Last Ranch

Ntonio Rodríguez Rivera was the unreliable son. Never good at arithmetic, but somehow good at remembering his prayers to the Virgin of Good Health. He'd spent sixteen of his nineteen years at Los Ojuelos attempting to replace his dead father and outdo his brothers. But it was 1858, and the Indians were giving the white folks trouble when Antonio's mother, Leocadia, unceremoniously threw him out of the house.

Her Indian servant Tomasa and the boy everyone knew as Joselito came to his room at five with his clothing in a bag and a bowl full of beans.

'Don't you *dare* think of taking the good woolen blanket we brought up from Brownsville,' Mama Leocadia said to him. The wool blanket had been carefully traded with the whites, but he was to have her old horse blanket, the one with small holes. 'That's my only good one and I want it for the baby that's coming.'

She shivered. 'It's quite cold for December, don't you think?' She tossed another log into the fire, wrapped her shawl around her shoulders. He splashed ice-cold water on his face. He wrapped the blanket around himself and stood in the doorway.

'My son, you look quite pathetic.' She folded her hands. 'It would be more beneficent to give you the good blanket, would it not?' She wrapped her blanket around his shoulders.

Leocadia was not known to be cruel, but times were tough: her oldest's baby was on the way, and there were not enough tortillas to go around on the ranch anymore.

Joselito gave him a couple of pesos.

'For the pains of the road,' he said. 'Don't give it all away, you know.'

Antonio, still rubbing the sleep out of his eyes, quickly pocketed them. He knew it would not be good money. Tomasa handed him the only fine thing she had ever owned: the mother-of-pearl rosary that Santa Anna's cousin had given to her during a semi-official visit long ago. That was when Texas was still Mexico, when the land was still virginal, untouched, in all its brushy desolation, when the wind was colder and the arrival of the autumn winds would bring the Lipan at the front door. Leocadia had just sold off another *porción* on the river to the whites—a bearded man named Schiller who had the bluest eyes he'd ever seen. He had a young wife who didn't care for Mexicans, or for Blacks, and had looked apprehensively or with disgust at Leocadia while she signed the papers. In return, Schiller gave her $200. It was the most they'd made in something like a hundred years.

A hundred years. The ranch was already 100 years old, and it had not been changed. There were certainties at Los Ojuelos: it was either hot and humid, or cold and windy. The missal had been laid out in the family chapel with the Virgin's picture that morning. He didn't know how old the family missal was. All he knew was that it was December the eighth.

Finally Mamá Leocadia came out with a bag of gold. It was six and she was dressed in black like she was ready to go to town.

'Take this, so that you won't be hungry. And for the love of God, buy some new clothes when you get to San Miguel.'

'I will, Mamá.'

'Joselito will take you past the gate. Don't bother coming back, because there won't be any room for you if you do.'

Antonio nodded and cast his eyes down. She was a formidable woman, his mother; she could tell she was anxious and upset that she'd have to let her youngest ones go, but these were hard times.

'Don't let the *bolillos* rob you. There are many unscrupulous people around these parts.'

'I won't, Mamá... I can't even see you for Christmas? Not even Easter?'

Leocadia thought for a moment. 'Christmas and Easter, yes. You can write to Padre Martínez and we can come and fetch you in the carriage.' She relaxed a little. '*Of course* you can come back; just because I cannot keep you here does not mean you may not visit.'

She tried not to sob when Joselito brought out the horse, but instead kept her voice as firm as possible, as firm as his father had often admonished them all to be in times like this.

'Go on,' Mamá Leocadia said. 'You'll travel to the visita that used to belong to the Aragón family. They have a house there but I'm not sure if anyone lives there anymore. But there is nothing but God's country beyond that.'

He looked back at her as Joselito closed the gate. He turned the other way, toward the west, where the clouds were beginning to break and the first patches of blue sky could be seen.

Antonio Rodríguez never saw his mother alive again after that.

Rather than console himself with his tears, he focused on the road. A family tradition held that the road to the Aragón ranch was some ten leagues long, more or less about a day's journey. Gradually, the road spiraled out from Los Ojuelos, into the vast expanse of the brushland, and soon Antonio smelled the new mown hay smell of woodruff and dust and brush. The road stretched out in a long line that rose up and over the low hills, past what used to be the church, whose rock wall now was now a stub on the side of the road studded with a few rude crosses, memories of a churchyard.

At about the second mile, Joselito stopped his horse.

Sereno

'Amigo mío, may God bless you.' He tipped his straw hat, roused the mare into a soft gallop, and turned toward home.

Antonio was alone—at the mercy of bandits from the other side, or Indians, or the whites' guns and their scalp hunters.

Toward four the sun had broken through the clouds and illuminated the brushland. It was bone-dry, a white forest of low and broken branches occasionally punctuated by the odd shape of a honey mesquite swarming with bees. Antonio found the rams that would escape from the Aragón's pasture tangled in the brambles of the brush during certain country walks, their fleece caught in the thorns of the plant called *corona de Cristo*. There were no rams now, but up on the side of the road, about a mile past the ruined chapel, he saw the white stone *pila* of the Aragón ranch, sticking out like a knife that had been thrown into the earth.

The Aragones were good people. Strong people. Silent people. They had known Antonio's family for years. Now things were different. After the War with the whites, they took horses, land, money—even Indians—for themselves, and wanted to bring their slaves to work the land. But the land would not give itself over to them, so they took what they could. The whites took Mexican wives to make half-breed babies that Mamá Leocadia said would be better off in God's glory than here on earth. *Because the people were sinning,* she said, God had cursed the earth with drought. Nearly everything died the summer before: the sheep, the lambs, the cows, the oxen, the chickens, the Indians, even his father, who died of the sweating fever. The fever was everywhere—it did not respect man nor woman, man nor beast, Indian nor white, Mexican nor American.

They sinned, so we pay for it?

Why do we have to pay for it? Antonio had once asked his mother.

Because, she said, *we always pay for it.*

The Aragones had paid for it too. Lost a daughter and a grandchild to the fever. The next summer, another baby, and the Indians came knocking. Señora Aragón bribed them with cornbread, but they wanted guns and horses. They killed her, her oldest son-in-law, his wife, made off with the baby. Weeks afterward, broken wedding china lay on the ground and the flies were still buzzing in the corral around pools of dried blood.

This was never how it was supposed to be.

Sereno

The front door of the house was off its hinges and leaned against the cool white walls. The porch was low and its roof covered with dried palm fronds. Antonio peeked in. No one had been living here for a while. The weak winter sun passed through the broken windows of the house, and the wind ran up the stairs to the second story. Antonio heard ghost stories but he had never seen a house that was a ghost--white as a sheet, its eyes gouged out by shotguns and arrows, rattling with dried beans and lentils, hollow like the trunk of an old cactus, filled with the skins of snakes and spiders. But here it was. The cradle was on the second story, turned over. The walls were still splashed with blood.

He went downstairs and into the pasture. The pasture was broad, flat: a plain of shortgrass. A trail ran back down to the rocky escarpment that abutted the stinking river that cut the land in two. The Indians had gone back into Mexico and left a trail of burnt beans and shells behind them. Antonio walked back toward his horse, brought him to the corral, and closed the gate. The horse looked at Antonio, as if he was expecting to be abandoned.

Toward the back of the house Antonio found the well, surprisingly pristine, its wellhead intact. A pail hung on a stick next to it. He watered his horse in the stone corral, and took a pail of water into the house to see if he could find a repast for that evening. By four-thirty the sun had disappeared behind a grey bank of clouds, the night was falling, and Antonio was cooking a handful of lentils in the pot on a fire in the kitchen. From the grey clouds came a few flakes of snow. After dinner, Antonio found tallow candles on the second floor in an overturned dresser; he righted it and set on it his rosary and hat, and in what used to be the bed that the Aragones slept in, he threw his blanket over him and ate his lentils in the dark.

'Antonio, wake up,' a voice called to him.

He turned over on his side and faced the wall.

The fire crackled.

'Antonio.'

'What? Don't disturb me now, I'm sleeping,' he said.

Sereno

He smelled beans cooking. It was a familiar smell. He smelled cornbread, the smell of butter and honey. Who was making pan de campo?

'Come and get some breakfast, Antonio.'

He shifted the blanket off his legs. The room was warm. The woman's voice sounded familiar. Maybe someone from church.

He turned over.

The woman. There she was. Brown skin, brown eyes. Turquoise ring. Someone familiar. Unfamiliar. A cameo hanging at her brown neck. American crinoline. Perfect, clipped Spanish.

'Good morning,' she said.

'Who are you? I thought no one lived here.'

'I live here. You know me. We used to play together.'

'From Los Ojuelos? I played with you?'

'Remember when we used to go down by the spring together, to fetch water together?'

The Last Ranch

In an instant Antonio remembered the plash of ice-cold water on his brown knees, the pleasant rush of dipping the wooden bucket into the water to retrieve a bucketful for the hogs. Her white dress, her exposed shoulders. The way the mesquite trees used to brush her cinnamon-skin shoulders. Black pussy bow and the same cameo locket.

'Lucia,' he said.

She nodded. Yes, that was her name.

A log in the fire cracked in two and embers spilled onto the flagstone.

'Do you want a glass of brandy?' she asked.

Lucía Aragón. He had indeed seen her, just a couple of times. Christmas. Easter. When the Padre had buried her. Small black coffin. A dead baby in her arms.

'Lucía Aragón? But you were dead.'

'No', she said. 'Not dead. The baby is not dead. My baby is alive, is with mamá grande in San Miguel. My husband is dead, but not me. My husband is buried in San Miguel.'

Sereno

'I could have sworn I went to your funeral.'

'No, no,' she said. 'You know me. We saw each other. You want some more chocolate? Have as much as you want.'

She poured a cupful of milk into his cup. He drank the milk. The cold wind blew through the chink through the door. She'd cleaned the house in the dead of the night, swept up the ashes, put food on the table, drew water, and washed the blood off the walls.

'But they killed your father, he said to her. They killed your mother and father. And I heard they killed you, killed your baby.'

'Yes,' she replied. 'I buried him with my hands.' She showed him the hands that dug up hard rocks and fought off a rattlesnake. 'You see that cairn out back? I dug it.'

In the afternoon, Antonio went to see the cairn. He tried peering down through the stones to see if there were any bodies in there, a skull grinning back at him from the cold earth. He saw nothing but stones. She walked out to show him where the cairns were. The grey earth, the yellow grass, the grey sky. Her warm hand pulsed in his. She put a woolen blanket over his shoulders, reminded her that he had traded this blanket with the whites six years ago. Had waved away mosquitoes with it.

'But how'd you find it?' he asked her.

'Your mother gave it to me.'

Lucía had seen Mamá Leocadia a handful of times. Had anticipated Antonio's coming to this house, she told him. He was not going to stay, he reminded her. Had to get to San Miguel, had to settle.

'No, stay here with me,' Lucía said. 'I'll take care of you. You don't have to leave. I live alone and I can manage myself.'

For dinner she made corn porridge and stewed a roast. There was enough food to feed three or four men.

'You have other men here?' he asked her. 'How do you have fresh meat in the middle of winter?'

'Sometimes they come, but they never stay. They'll usually drop things off. I can live off of very little. Sometimes I eat.'

'How'd you survive the Indians coming to take everything you have?' he asked her.

'I prayed to the Virgin to hide me in the brush.' She closed her eyes. He watched her hands tell the story. 'She scooped me up off from the Indian's horse. For three afternoons I stared up at the sky, watching the colors change, watching the clouds. Fearing death from a rattlesnake. The moon. The devil. You name it,' she said.

Lucía belonged to the fuzzy sunlit past. Had been married to a man named Julián, whom the Lipan bisected with arrows. Split his head down the middle with a pickaxe. Threw the baby on the walls of the house, slit Lucía's throat and swabbed the face of the father against the ground until nothing was left.

In his dream he saw thunder. In his dream Lucía was at the metate rolling corn into masa. He saw the thunder billow into the house, topple over the jugs, watched the water spill and spread in great red puddles. Saw Lucía working her masa into balls. She was making tortillas when the Lipan got to her. He saw her scream, her mouth full of blood. But she was alive now.

The Last Ranch

In his dream, she hovered above him in her Scots crinoline. He saw the white soles of her feet, her white petticoats, her shawl suspended in air. An aureole of blue light surrounded her, as if she was being assumed into heaven. When he turned around, he looked in the mirror and saw his back quivering with arrows, like a javelina that had been shot through. When he woke, she was sitting on a chair beside the bed, with coffee and corn porridge and chili.

'You must tell me how you survived,' he said to her.

She smiled gently. 'By the grace of God.'

It was dark outside again. He thought it might rain.

'God saved me. He hid me in the *incienso* bushes. I was getting water for Daddy's horse and they found me. So I ran. I kept running until I couldn't run anymore. Threw the bucket out so they'd think I ran somewhere else. I ran down to the river and waded into the water and stayed there, with my head under the water until it was all right to come back.'

'And you didn't drown?'

She shook her head.

'No, I would bob my head up. I swam back and forth until sunset.'

Antonio had been at the wake. He'd seen her laying in the coffin in her white dress and veil. Her body was riddled with stab wounds. Alone her face the Lipan had preserved. Fresh and virginal, like a lily of May. Women had perfumed her body with orange blossoms, had stuffed the dried orange blossom bouquet—from her wedding—into her stiff hands.

He went out to see if the soil on Lucia's land was fertile.

He could pull up only bones.

Animal bones, human bones.

He walked back to the house.

'You haven't thought about planting soon?' he said. The ground needs tilling.'

'When we get to the new year, we'll dig up the ground, you and me. I can get a man to come out and help us.'

'There isn't a man living between here and Los Ojuelos. Unless it's my family you're talking about.'

She nodded. 'Yes, your family. Or maybe even you. You ride back and get your plough.'

'We can plough the land together, sow some corn and beans. We can make this place ours.'

'We aren't even married,' he said.

'Yes, but I want to be married again,' she replied.

'But you're a widow.'

'I know I am a widow,' she said. 'But I am a young widow.'

The girl in San Miguel he'd written to had been promised to him, but he had no idea what she looked like. The family didn't have enough for a miniature to be sent, and they'd never been properly introduced before Mamá Leocadia had told Antonio to leave Los Ojuelos.

Sereno

Lucía was beautiful. Lucía's brown eyes that shimmered like sapphires, with their strange fire.

Antonio wanted to kiss Lucía, pull her into bed with him. Her perfume lingered on her arms, a strange fragrance of orange blossom and holy water. He could feel her staring at him when he turned his back to her, when he changed out of his shirt.

That evening, she drew him a bath. Bade him to strip and sit in a tub full of steaming, warm water. She scrubbed his hands, ran her fingers through his hair, placed a hand on his chest and gently rubbed the slippery soap into his brown skin. He leaned back and closed his eyes. She inclined her head and she planted a kiss. In her warm kiss was a touch of ice, a touch of the grave, the taste of horseflesh and alum. He opened his eyes and she was gone.

She sat at the other end of the room, shaking the pan of coals.

'Tomorrow we'll kill the bedbugs,' she said.

She handed him a white sheet.

'Put this around yourself and cover up. Sit by the fire.'

The Last Ranch

He sat on a low stool and felt the warmth of the fire stir himself up. He wanted to mount her on the ground, feel himself inside of her, strip her down and kiss her breasts, wanted to feel her breasts in his hands. But instead she made him dinner and watched him eat it.

'Do you believe in fate?' she asked him, pouring him a cup of wine.

'I believe in fate. But also in God's will.'

'I believe in fate,' she said to him.

A week passed and he did not stir from the house. He went out every morning and fed his horse. In San Miguel, he told himself, he would sell the horse and get a new one. She was an old nag, she needed to be put to pasture. But on this morning, the horse lay in the field. Someone had come in the night and cut its head off and skinned it alive, pulled out its entrails, devoured them. A mass of maggots swarmed inside the cavity.

'You'll get another one,' Lucía said.

'With what money?' Antonio replied, heartbroken. 'You want me to *walk* to San Miguel?'

'You'll get another one,' she kept saying. 'Go out to the well and look down in it.'

He looked at her as if she was telling a lie. Her face was serious, unfazed by the stench of carrion.

'You don't believe me,' she said.

'Where do you come from? Where do you think money comes from, huh? Do you think I could just pull it out of the ground?'

She walked back into the house and closed the door.

He walked to the well. Looked into the well. Looked and squinted. The sun came out and shone into the very black hole. He glanced down once and saw a pair of eyes looking up from the dark. He looked down again. Nothing.

He sent down a bucket into the bottom of the well. When he pulled the bucket out, it was full of gold pieces.

He walked back into the house and found her wiping her hands at the table on a tablecloth.

'You weren't lying,' he replied. 'I owe you an apology.'

'If you want to stay here,' she said, 'You must trust me when I tell you these things.'

'So you want me to believe that you survived the Lipan burning your house down? Did you survive or not? I saw your body in the bier. I saw them bury you.'

'I am alive,' she said. She showed him her fleshy hands, took a pointed knife and pricked her finger. Stood up and showed him her finger, made him kiss the blood. She did not take her eyes off of him. He tasted the iron of her blood.

'I am alive,' she said, over and over again. 'I am living.'

The days blurred. The sky was a blank canvas. Sometimes it looked grey, other days it was bright blue with long bands of white that turned pink at sunrise and sunset. Lucía didn't talk too much, but she did a lot of looking. At four o'clock the sky would dim and things would start turning blue. Lucía would come in with a cord of wood for the fire. She kept the fire burning all night, tossing a log in, watching the sparks fly up the chimney and dance on the flagstones. Not once did an ember dare to catch on her crinoline. She sat on her settee and embroidered all night and listened to his stories.

'What ever became of your cousin Rodrigo,' she said. 'You had mentioned him once.'

'In Camargo,' he said. 'Just married a German girl. I don't know her name and from what I hear she doesn't speak a word of Spanish. Can you imagine that? Coming to a country you've never been to and expecting to learn a language you've never heard?'

'I suppose we could ask the whites that question.'

He smiled, chuckled a little, stared into the fire.

'What's that you're embroidering?'

'Something pretty,' Lucía responded. 'Something you'll like.'

He got up out of bed, put his hands on her shoulders. She was warm like he was, warmed by the fire and by the genial conversation.

'Show me how far you've come along in your embroidery.'

'All right,' she said, and turned down a leaf of fabric.

Instead of petit point flowers, she was embroidering a scene: the Lipan on horseback burning the house and splitting her husband's head wide open. The baby was on the ground, a trampled mess of blood and entrails, embroidered in pink and scarlet threads.

The next morning he got up early. Lucía lay asleep in the bed. The first blue light of the cold morning was beginning to peek through the naked windowpane. He pulled on his long johns and trousers and boots and snuck outside.

He walked. Kept walking until he spied a fire on a distant hill. Kept walking until the smoke plume was no longer a distant wisp of grey smoke in the blue sky. The frost crunched under his boots. Under the billowing pillar, he saw a white man burning a cart full of what looked like old clothing.

'Who are you?' the old white man said. '*I no tango aquas akee.*'

'No quiero água,' Antonio replied. 'Need a horse.'

The old white man's face blanched and he pulled out a pistol.

'Chinga tu madre, boy. I don't got no goddamn horse except the one I fought for. I'm not gonna let you be the one to best me for it.'

He cocked the pistol.

'I'm sorry, I am asking for help, I am not a bad man,' Antonio replied.

'Bullshit, son,' the old man replied. 'Now git on, I don't have the patience to put up with Mexicano sons-of-bitches on my goddamn land.'

The burning cart, Antonio realized, was full of the personal effects of Cayetano Lerda, his next-door neighbor. This was his land. And if it was indeed Cayetano's land, the river was not far off.

'Git on,' the old man said, pushing him back toward the road. Antonio walked back to the house, bewildered, afraid. He could not stay at Lucía's house, and his neighbors were not the same. 'Don't you come back here, you hear?'

'I need a horse,' Antonio said. 'I must be leaving some day. I'm running out of time and money.'

'I can give you anything you want here,' Lucía said. 'I am telling you that you do not even have to leave for Mexico. Stay with me and be my husband.'

'Lucía,' Antonio replied, pushing off Lucía's warm brown hands, 'I am given to someone else. I am promised to someone else.'

'How do you know she wants you?' Lucía replied, coolly. 'She could be dead of cholera for all you know. She could resting in her coffin right now and you wouldn't even know. When was the last time you heard from her? October, wasn't it?'

'How did you know that?'

Lucía wrapped her shawl around her and took up her embroidery again. 'October. And it's December now.

And you don't live at Los Ojuelos. You don't live anywhere except for here. So I don't know what to tell you, then.'

Antonio felt defeated. He knelt at her feet and looked up into her eyes. She continued to embroider.

'I am the only living thing you know. The only woman who loves you. Your house is my house. I am yours. Don't leave me again.'

The frost came on hard that night and iced the window panes. Lucía unveiled herself before Antonio and she had become a luminous brown flame that burned itself into Antonio's slim frame. He'd never been with a woman before. Had never savored a woman, even in sin. But Lucía was no whore. She was precious and immune to the world, yet she knew everything, felt everything, could feed him and keep him warm and bathe him. They made love before the flagstones of the hearth and as the fire roared before them he felt her fingertips and tiny embers burn into his buttocks. She could not be a ghost, for ghosts couldn't love. She had to have been an angel in this, the house of the dead, a messenger, a blithe spirit, some living memory of the past.

The Last Ranch

The fire died down and he stared at the ceiling. The moon was shining through the window panes and had caught the bottom of a ceramic bowl sitting on the kitchen table. Such beautiful blue and white light. Moonlight in winter, that special type of moonlight that illuminated everything. The wind rushed through the chink of the doorway. The chill north wind rattled the door until it rustled against the jamb.

Antonio felt her warm breasts, her breath on his, their legs intertwined. He closed his eyes and savored it. He opened them again and there, staring back at him from the ceiling, was a baby in the moonlight, smiling and laughing, clapping its pale hands. Up the wall ran a track of bloody baby footprints.

Dear Padre I am writing to you because I am late and not feeling well I have been staying in the house of one Lucía Aragón who I am very sure was killed by the Apaches last year but has survived apparently You must understand dear Padre that I have not forgotten about María & that I intend to marry her as soon as I arrive but my arrival has been delayed somewhat by the circumstances which I am about to relate

'You were dreaming.'

Sereno

'I was not, I assure you,' Antonio said. 'I'm getting out of here.'

He pulled his woolen poncho off the wall and wrapped it around his body. He put on his sombrero and shouldered his bag. If the horses would not come to him, he would go to the horses. With the gold he'd pulled in from the well.

'It is too dangerous out there,' Lucía said. 'You'll die if you leave.'

'If I stay here, madam, I will be sure to go mad,' Antonio replied.

He opened the door. Sunlight warmed on his face as he stepped out of the house. The blue sky stretched out before him.

Down over the hills came a multitude of figures clothed in what looked skins. They came on horseback and on foot, and Antonio could see their scowls emerge through the thickets of low brush. A few volleys popped off in white puffs of smoke against the brilliant blue sky.

He smiled incredulously as if he was watching some sort of strange farce play out in front of him.

The Last Ranch

Antonio saw brown faces, scowls, heard the jingle of shells, saw the fringe of short coats. Three Apaches advanced forward, one drawing a bow.

Antonio heard the flick of the arrow as it landed in his skull. Another man rushed past him into the house. Antonio fell to his knees. He fell back against the wall of the house, struggled to reach back inside, just past the lintel of the door.

The house was coming apart inside: jars of dry beans shattered, Lucía screamed, crumbs of bread flew, the fire roared out of the fireplace, the beams caught fire and moaned, the adobe buckled, the roof caved in.

The horses trampled Antonio's body, broke his arms and his legs, and tore off the linen shirt he'd been wearing. He curled into a ball against the wall of the burning house. The sky dimmed to midnight and he closed his eyes in death.

In her moonlight crinoline, Lucía advanced toward him with open arms, a skeletal Lucía, whose pale white bones were like the white of her shift the first day that he had plunged his hands into the water at Los Ojuelos, mortal Lucía whose gaze was the color of cold water and the night, whose breath was carrion and the sweet taste of orange blossom water.

Saint Godelieve

THEY SAY THAT WHEN THE LORD allowed Saint Godelieve's body to be found, the night fog had settled over the stinking pond wherein she'd been drowned, in order to cover her nakedness. They said the Lord Himself covered her dead body with a cloud. You see, the people already knew she was a saint. It didn't matter what her husband Bertolf or his mother said, or what the Bishop of Tournai and Soissons said, or even what her father said, who had complained to Count Eustace himself, who washed his hands of the entire affair.

Ask people like me to tell you what a saint looks like. You don't need a fat friar to tell you. I'll show you.

The poor waited for her at the back of the big house. In the dead of night, she had handed loaves of warm bread and cups of sweet spiced wine to these poor people. Even when she was being starved to punish her, she still managed to convince the cook to let her feed them. The people say angels fed her in return. Her unfinished bowl of barley and lentils was a feast to those who had begged

God for even a half-chewed morsel from the master's table.

'But don't tell anyone you saw me,' she would say to me. 'You didn't see me, and if anyone asks you where you got this food, just say the sisters gave it to you. And be sure to thank The Lord for it, after you're done.'

I stood before her in my cambric shirt, unrepentant and discalced. I was 11 years old and I'd begged all day in the rain. I sat there on the step of the master's kitchen with the other kids, licking a wooden bowl, rubbing a last crumb of bread into it to sop up the last trickle of lentil soup.

'But you must learn your sacraments, all of you,' she whispered. 'Say your prayers tonight before bed. Pray for me, and the animals, and the master, too. Pray for all of us.'

Every so often we'd see Bertolf's awful mother Lydwina, who scowled at us from her fat grey mare and tried to scatter us whenever she rode by our house. We'd come out to say hello and she'd sneer and hold her nose.

'Don't you people have anything better to do?' she say. 'You live like swine, all of you. How shameful.'

Saint Godelieve

She'd look at our hovel, our house of birch thatch and wood, at my poor mother and our baby sister, and shake her head.

'You two smell like a sty,' she said to me and my brother. 'Don't you ever take a bath? If your poor father had the good mind to stop playing with himself, maybe the Good Lord might've shown you all a bit of kindness.'

All of that abuse for just a glance at Godelieve, riding to church with Bertolf and his awful mother. They'd ride through the wheat fields, up and over the hill, toward the church with its steeple. I followed close behind them, gathering poppies and bachelor's buttons to make crowns for me and my brothers, and I'd watch Godelieve's white veil fly like a banner in the wind. At Mass she was a white butterfly caught in the cold stone box of the church. My eyes coveted her hands—they were fine and unblemished, her fingers pale and tender-looking. She always looked so intent at prayer. She wasn't praying, I thought, maybe she was thinking about something else. Maybe she does embroidery, there in her cell in the big house. Maybe she draws or paints. Maybe she reads. *Does a lady like Godelieve know how to read? Do they let her read, do you think?* I'd say to my brother. *What sort of books do you think they let her read?*

Sereno

The day after the people found her, a constable galloped past the house on the way to the big house. The sun disappeared behind a thunderhead. Soon the bell tolled from the church, once, twice, three times.

'It's going to hail,' my mother said. 'I can feel it in my bones.'

All us kids were out in the field, looking at the slate sky, tinged with green. Lightning cracked in the west and the thunder rolled out long and hard against the hard earth of July.

'The Lord is going to smite all of you if you don't come in and peel these rutabagas,' my mother said, slamming the door.

My next-door neighbor Willem had run through the storm to let us know the awful news. We were warming ourselves by the fire, and my mother tried in vain to rock my sister to sleep. We were shocked into silence.

'None of us know who did it,' he said. 'She was asleep when they took her, though. They led her toward the pasture and threw her in the mill pond.'

Saint Godelieve

'Absolutely dreadful,' my mother said. 'And her father doesn't know?'

'Not a thing,' Willem replied. 'The old woman who lives at the end of the road told me she saw the body.'

'I wouldn't be surprised it if it was the mother-in-law,' Mother said.

'Isn't it *always* the mother-in-law?' Willem replied.

We were gathering up the gleanings of the wheat harvest in the sunset. The heat broke over us like a cracked egg and sizzled on our backs.

'How'd you know her?' the old man said, bending down to tie his shoe.

'She gave me a bunch of carrots and onions for Easter,' the old woman replied. 'And for Ascension Day, she sent me a rabbit. I never had rabbit before, but she said the cooks made too much in the master's kitchen.'

'That had to have been a lie. Maybe she stole the rabbit from the kitchen before it was to be served. Maybe that's why they killed her. Because she was a thief.'

'Well now, that wouldn't make sense, now, would it? Robbing the rich to feed the poor? What makes you think she would have had that much freedom? Lydwina had kept her clapped up in her bedroom. For her own safety, she said. I heard it from her very own lips one Christmas.'

'You're fibbing, Margaret! I just know you are.'

'No, no!' the old woman replied, laughing in a dry gasp. 'I heard it as plain as day.'

It thundered that evening, but no rain came. A couple of constables rode by us again, followed by a messenger from the Bishop of Tournai and Soissons, in a red cape and a very funny looking hat. After supper, we went walking into town to gather up what was left on the ground at the market. Lord Bertolf's house was all lit up inside. Smoke rose from the chimney. The cooks had thrown blood and dung on the ground behind the kitchen and for a moment I thought they had butchered Godelieve, cut her up to pickle her. Out came Lydwina, looking cranky. She saw my youngest brother picking barley groats out of the mud.

'Good God in Heaven,' Lydwina said, rushing over to my brother. 'Don't you people have any shame?'

My mother inclined her head. Lydwina picked my brother up and smeared off the mud from his mouth.

'Good evening, my lady.'

'Save your pleasantries for church, Barbara,' Lydwina says. 'Don't you know how shameful it is to have your youngest stoop in the mud for food from the master's table? When all you could have done was ask.'

'Forgive me, my lady Lydwina, I—'

'Don't say anything to me. You've always gotten under my skin, Barbara, did you know that? Always in church, looking helpless and needy as ever. Didn't anyone ever tell you God gave you hands in which to work?'

Lydwina set my brother on the ground and wiped her hands with a white handkerchief.

'Listen to me very carefully. I want your eldest to come and attend me tomorrow morning. I want to hear no protests whatsoever. I'll give you as much food as you like for him. You look like you could stand to have one less child tugging at your apron strings.'

Sereno

My mother shrunk under Lydwina's monstrous gaze. I thought Lydwina would snap at any moment.

'The days of wanton excess have ended here on Lord Bertolf's land. From now on all of us will have to work our fingers to the bone to make sure we all eat.'

'My lady—'

'Don't you listen to orders? What a stupid woman you are.'

'I'm terribly sorry, my lady.'

'Don't apologize. Get all of your whelps to the master's kitchen. Have old Pieter feed all of them. You can tell him I said it was alright to do so. And for the love of Almighty God, Barbara, wash your face. You're a widow, don't you forget about that.'

Old Lydwina laid an awful glance at us once more, and then turned back toward the steps to the big house. After she was gone, Pieter, the master's cook, had us all sit at a long table. He ladled rich broth into wooden bowls and gave us some crusty rye bread. All of us had the first semblance of a good meal in more than three months.

Saint Godelieve

I would not be the one to scare away the crows in the corn the next morning. Instead, my mother prodded me out of bed and walked me to the gate of the big house. We held hands and walked up the slippery steps together. The guard at the post looked suspicious.

'My lady Lydwina has asked that I bring my eldest. She has need of him.'

'So you've been selected to be an errand boy,' the guard replied, looking at me. I didn't reply. 'He doesn't have anything that would cause trouble, right?'

My mother looked down at me.

'You got rid of the slingshot, didn't you, son?'

I nodded. The guard laughed and for a moment I saw the gap in his yellowed teeth.

'Go right in,' he said, chuckling. 'And behave yourself.'

The gate opened and my mother loosened her grip on my hand.

'Go on, my son, they're waiting for you.'

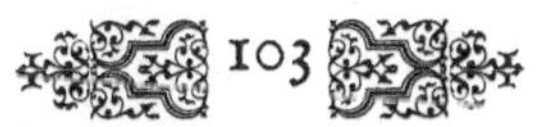

Sereno

The barbican gate lowered. I looked back. My mother watched me through the grille.

Godelieve had been nothing like Lydwina. Where Lydwina was cruel and stone-faced, Godelive was cheerful and generous. I thought she was especially pretty. She smelled of roses and newly mown hay. Every Sunday afternoon, she appeared at our front door, basket under an arm, bearing gifts. She brought peaches and greengages from the orchard. Plums and apples in September from her father's lands. The good nuns would send loaves of bread and bags of barley and oats through her. Every poor person on Lord Bertolf's land could eat well because of Godelieve. There were, of course, murmurings that her generosity had caused the count money troubles. That's what they said about her when she lived with her father, Hemfrid. Her mother Ogiva tried to marry her off to the highest bidder, but Godelieve wouldn't budge. 'Make me a nun', she said. But instead of making her a nun, they made her marry—or rather, Eustace, Count of Boulogne, made her marry— his nephew, Bertolf, lord of Ghistelles. And so instead of roaming the halls of some nunnery, she roamed the fields with me on Sunday afternoons, while we scared away crows pecking at the ripe grain.

Saint Godelieve

Once, when she held hands with me while Mother and Father showed her their poor plot of land, she prayed, 'Would to God I'd have become a nun! So that I could give you all of my money and you wouldn't ever have to worry about feeding your family ever again.' I ran in the fields with Godelieve, showed her how to drive off crows and sparrows with my slingshot. I wanted to play hide-and-go-seek in the forest behind Lord Bertolf's lands, and pretend I was Merlin and she was Nimue and we were in search of the Holy Grail. She rocked me to sleep under a robur oak with her stories of the martyrs. But now she was gone. I had my first real job, and the memory of her face was fading fast.

Not too long after she died, people started saying a great light could be seen in the still evenings, usually right after sundown. No one I knew saw this light, though lots of people had been by the mill-pond after Godelieve's body was found. The people said angels' footprints could be seen on the path where those barbarians had killed her.

Maybe it was the Jews that killed her, someone said. *You know how the Jews are: ravenous, bloodthirsty. They killed The Lord, don't you know!* But no one had known what a

Jew looked like in Ghistelles then. Someone else said it was her cousin, a suitor who had been reproved by the Bishop because he was in one degree of affinity too close to be married. But if you asked me and the other people in town who it was that had Godelieve killed, we all could have told you it was either Lydwina or the Count himself.

I never liked the Count. Even in youth, he looked weak, blighted by disease. Too skinny. Looked and smelled too much like a wet chicken. If only he'd have complained less, things would have been fine. But the two of them came and went together in pairs: like thunder and lightning, needle and thread, bread and butter, Bertolf and Lydwina. Everywhere they went they complained, harangued, endlessly argued with whomever was unlucky to be in their path.

'Don't let yourself be alone with the master,' the laundry maid told me one day. 'He'll eat you up alive.'

'You're kidding me,' I replied.

'Now look here, boy,' the laundry maid said, suddenly offended. 'I'm being serious. Lord Bertolf skinned one cat, he'll skin you. And don't let Lady

Lydwina know that you've been in his chambers or you're gonna get it, just you wait.'

'These are very serious charges, I hope you understand. You stand accused of having committed an outrage,' the Bishop's messenger said to Lord Bertolf and Lydwina that morning in the great hall. Before them both lay a large white sheet on a table.

'The wife of a nobleman is someone to be respected and trusted. According to what my servant Henry told my lord the Bishop, some person with few scruples took Godelieve in the dead of night down toward the mill-pond, strangled her with the sheet you see before you, and then cast her body into the water.'

'And you are sure that they have no other accomplices?' Lady Lydwina said.

'Of that, my lady, I am assured.'

'And you have come, then, to draw us away?'

'No,' the messenger replied. 'I've come to inform you that the Bishop has indicated that he intends to pay a visit to determine if... well, to determine if you had anything to do with the death of this young woman.'

The count pulled out his sword from its hilt and pointed it at the messenger.

'I'll cut you into so many pieces the crows won't know where to begin!' Lord Bertolf cried out.

The messenger moved the sword away from his throat with two fingers.

'*First* of all,' the messenger said, 'Let's not be rash here. I have read the warrant. Whoever did this will forfeit their lives. The Bishop is prepared to apply a dispensation to my lord and lady in lieu of a formal act of repentance.'

'What have *I* done?' Lydwina said. 'What makes you think *I* should be asking the Bishop, or anyone else for that matter, for forgiveness?'

'You know perfectly what you've done, let's not be cute. The rumor of your treatment of my late lady has been the talk of the town.'

Saint Godelieve

Lord Bertolf hilted his sword. 'She had her reasons. We were in a crisis. Godelieve was giving away goods from the manor to the poor at an excessive rate.'

'And you ran her off, didn't you? Lord Hemfrid told me that you'd wooed her with promises that you'd end her immurement in her chambers. The Bishop is very much concerned that your ill treatment compromised the religious vows she took as wife.'

'You are mistaken,' Lydwina replied. 'I *loved* my daughter-in-law. You are all wrong. I would have *never* wanted this to happen. At *all*.'

'You can tell the Bishop I'll answer his questions, but by God, he's crazy to think that I would be responsible for such an awful crime,' Bertolf said.

'God is not mocked,' the Bishop's messenger said. 'And neither will my lord the Bishop be. He expects you to be ready to meet him within two days or so. Put your minds and your house in order until then.'

As he was leaving the messenger looked at me while I stood by the door to the big house.

'It seems like quite a shame to me,' the messenger said, 'that you should have such young children working in a den of iniquity.'

'I'm am through with having to listen to your pronouncements of judgment on perfectly innocent people,' Lord Bertolf replied.

'Men like you never learn. Remember, my Lord, that you are in mourning. Your wife is dead. A woman like that is rare in these parts. Your indecency is galling. Put your thoughts in order.'

'But they're feeding you better, right? You look better. You look like you're doing well,' my mother said to me that evening. 'And you're saying your prayers at night?'

She was at the gate talking to me through the grille. It was market day and she had a basket full of turnips on her arm.

'Yes, mother, I am,' I replied. 'I don't get to sleep late, believe me...'

'I've been worried for you, my son. The rumor is that Bertolf mistreats his servants. I've been praying that God's mother protect you.'

I slipped a gold coin through the grille and into her hand.

'A week's wages,' I replied. 'So that you can buy some groceries.'

She closed her hand around the gold coin and smiled.

'Well, anyway, son. I've heard rumors, is all. Keep your eyes open. In a few days we'll come back to check up on you, me and your brothers and sisters.'

A few days later I was in Godelieve's room, a dry, drafty cold wooden closet at the end of the hall. There was a solitary chink in the wall, a needle that let in just a sliver of light and maybe the faintest whisper of wind. She had scrawled a large cross into the wall and under that some strange words. The wine steward, a short, thin man named Hacca, looked down at the mess Godelieve's murderers had made of her room.

'Those animals,' he kept saying. 'Just look at this. Blood and water spilled everywhere. Those barbarians. To treat my lady so.'

'What does that writing mean?' I asked.

Hacca stood up from where he was stooping and squinted his eyes at the inscription.

'It means, "have mercy on me, God". You hear it at Mass sometimes. A very odd thing to write on the wall of one's room.'

From the chink I could see the square below, and just past the gate, the steeple of the church, like the mast of a ship in a sea of grain.

They wrapped Godelieve's body in a white sheet and placed her coffin in the ground. We followed her funeral procession with torches and armfuls of wildflowers. I could divine only certain features through her shroud: her lips, her dark hair, her blue eyes, her fingertips which were ivory and which were now blue. All the girls of the big house—Godelieve's cousins and relatives, relatives I was forbidden to address—wept and threw armfuls of white flowers over her grave, and we all stood there under the hot sun our prayers scrambled in our brains like runny eggs. I never realized how close I had been to the stench of death. I had smelled it in carrion rotting on the master's land. I knew the smell of death, I tasted it. I could smell her fragrance of white flowers mingling with that of death. The perfume was intoxicating, mystifying. Handfuls of earth fell on her coffin of sticky pine--one after another, young and old, passing, amid the cries of girls and muffled sighs of old women. Men did not cry in those days--they shuffled along as they do now, unaware, a lost chorus of mourners, confused and alone, out of control.

'Come here, boy,' Lydwina said to me. I had prepared the fire for Lydwina and turned down her bed. It was raining. A cool wind was blowing in the hall. She placed her hands on my shoulders and looked at me intently.

'Do you believe in hell?'

'What's hell?

'Oh, it's a *terrible* place,' Lydwina replied. 'More horrible than you could possibly imagine. It's where malefactors go.'

'What's a malefactor?'

'It's a person who's done bad things. A criminal.'

'I'm sure I won't go to hell, then.'

'Are you so sure?' she whispered. 'How do you know?'

'My mother says that if I pray at night, God will listen to me and take me to heaven. So I pray every night that God's mother take me.'

Tears filled her eyes. 'And... what do you think about me? Do you think I'm going to hell?'

'No,' I replied.

Lydwina inclined her head, put her hands in her face, and wept.

I had seen the bishop's messenger, who looked like a strange creature in his cap of red velvet, but I had never met the bishop himself. The day he came to Ghistelles with his retinue the house buzzed with people. The bishop was lean, but he ate like he had just returned from war. A day and night I helped the kitchen to kill geese and chickens. Then the Count's men returned with a fat boar and we all stood there, wondering how in the world we would serve it.

'You'll have to burn off the hair first,' the kitchen maid Frideswide said.

'And then bleed it,' Editha said.

"I used to be a butcher for Count Eustace in England. I know how to kill and serve things around here. I say is that you skin a boar first, and eviscerate it.'

He thrust a knife into the boar's neck and ran it down through its chest and stomach. Blood and intestines fell to the kitchen floor.

'I have my suspicions,' Frideswide said, leaning to me and whispering to me under her breath.

'Pieter would have known how to kill. Since he was a butcher in England and all. '

'What makes you so sure?' I replied. 'She was drowned, not cut open.'

'Shh! You don't want him to notice, do you? Speak softer, child.'

Sereno

I lowered my eyes and returned to turning the spit. I watched the grease drip onto the hot hearth, flare up, drift away into the updraft of the chimney.

'I was there when they pulled her out. It was the most ghastly thing you ever saw. Pieter, though—he wasn't anywhere to be found that morning. Don't you think that a cook would know how to get rid of a body?'

'I was there when I saw those sons-of-whores take my lady. I thought I must have been having some sort of strange dream,' the laundry maid told me over supper that night. 'But you won't hear me utter a peep before the bishop or his men, no sir.'

'You should have said something, though,' I said.

'Naturally I wouldn't have,' Pieter said. 'I couldn't stand her. Her simpering face annoyed me. "Please pray for the souls lost in the world,", she used to say. Where's the common sense in a girl like that?'

'For some people,' the laundry maid then said, 'she was the only real chance for a warm meal.'

Saint Godelieve

'Oh please,' Pieter replied. 'People can work. You and me can work.'

The laundry maid cleared her throat and at once the table became quiet. Everyone was looking at me.

'Oh, so you were a beneficiary of her generosity, then?'

'She fed me and my family,' I replied.

'Well then,' Pieter replied, a little miffed. 'Then you can understand the considerable difficulty that placed on all of us.'

Frideswide the laundry maid pulled up a dingy white sheet out of a basket and stuffed into the cauldron. 'I'm sure you didn't hear about the witch the master saw.'

I rolled over the straw mat I lay on, unable to sleep.

'A witch?' Editha said. 'You believe in such things?'

'Oh, yes,' Frideswide said. 'How else do you think the Devil gets loose?'

'My mother, God rest her soul, used to say that those things are just fictions. You know, like the fairies or the gnomes. You couldn't possibly expect me to believe that, would you?'

'Bertolf saw an old woman in the next town over,' she said, stirring a long baton that she muddled laundry with. 'A tiny old thing. Folks are saying she was able to get one of the girls in town pregnant without her husband knowing her. Just had her go out to St Winnoc's well on a certain night, pick certain herbs, and then made her drink this potion.'

'What was in it?' Editha replied.

'Only God knows,' Frideswide said. 'I'm sure all sorts of awful things.'

'Did the potion work?'

'What do you think?'

'I'll believe it when I see it. Even if the master wanted to be close to my lady, he would have had a lot more sense than to go to witches to do that.'

'She was unbreakable,' Frideswide said. 'Like a dog to a bone on her love of God and the Church and all that.

What a waste. A girl that pretty, shut up in a convent for the rest of her life. Imagine losing all of that lovely dowry money to some dour abbess, so that she can read books and play the psaltery all day.'

In the morning I stood in the hall with the Bishop and the entire household lined up against the wall. Lord Bertolf sat alone on a stool in the middle of the hall, dwarfed by the Bishop, an old man in black and ermine robes.

'We were what you might call a normal couple,' Lord Bertolf began, rather sheepishly. 'She was from Boulogne. My mother swore up and down I'd rue the day I married a foreigner. But I suppose when you have officials to please and a good impression to make, you place these criticisms aside.'

'Go on,' The Bishop said.

Lord Bertolf coughed and put his hand up. 'I'm sorry—this is all very hard on me.'

'I'm fairly sure that your wife felt the same.'

Sereno

There was a jostling in the hall, a few muffled chuckles. The thick-necked Bishop cast a sly wink at his page, a pale, quivering boy who looked younger than me.

'Anyway—my mother said I'd end up regretting being married to Godelieve. Sure, we had our disagreements. This folly about her wanting to take vows, that was one disagreement. And the other folly, *feeding* people. *That* I had a problem with.'

'How so?'

'You see the weather. Hot and dry for a few days, then a storm comes and all the grain is trampled over. And then you begin to worry. I worry for my men who work the fields. We barely have enough to make to pay our way through the year and here she is throwing out loaves of bread to beggar children.'

'I don't see anything wrong with that.'

A few more chuckles. Bertolf looked hurt by this, poisoned by the Bishop's quiet rebuke.

'Was it true that you disappeared from your wedding party for three whole days?'

The Count's eyes widened. He stared down the bishop as if he had uttered a curse, and stood up from his stool.

'That's a lie. A bald-faced lie. I know who uttered it. It was Hemfrid.'

'That's not what I hear,' the Bishop replied. 'Your own servants informed me.'

'My father—God rest his soul—told me that, if I were to undertake marriage to Godelieve I'd never see the end of all of this religious frenzy. Monks and nuns rapping at my door, begging for money. Sick children begging with open hands for my table scraps. I did not so much have second thoughts,' he said, tightening his voice, 'as genuine concerns for the state of my household.'

He turned around to look at all of us.

'And when I find out which one of you opened your mouth to slander your master, God help you that I don't rip your tongue out with my own two hands.'

Sereno

The summer wind had stirred up a whirl of dust in the hall on the day that Lydwina spoke to the bishop.

'I regret my harshness,' Lydwina said. 'But my lord, you must understand the anxiety that this woman placed on me and my son. Is it not the example of God's Mother, our heavenly mother, to intercede on behalf of her children?'

'That is understandable,' the Bishop replied. 'When the cause is evidently one in God's favor. Lord Hemfrid and Lady Ogiva informed me that twice you dissuaded your son from marrying Godelieve, and that you expelled her from his house with a wooden shoe.'

'I lost my temper,' Lydwina said, her voice breaking, 'She had given a loaf of fine white bread and bean stew to two worthless beggars at the backdoor of the house. We had barely enough to feed ourselves.'

'Did you hit her with the shoe?'

She nervously swallowed and wiped with two fingers the sweat that had formed on her brow. She nodded and said nothing.

The bishop drank from his cup of wine and placed it on the tray held by the pale quivering page.

Saint Godelieve

'Did you coerce your servants to kill Godelieve?'

'No,' she said, shaken. 'Never in a thousand years would I think of killing her. I *loved* my daughter-in-law. Yes, we may have had difficulties, but I thought these could have been worked out. When I was eighteen my husband straightened me out. I put girlish things away. She was deluded with this sick fixation on helping people she thought were needy. But they aren't needy— just lazy.'

I watched the bishop wave away the page and close the door. He poured himself another cup of weak wine and sat down at his chair.

'Care to tell me more?' the Bishop replied.

The hot wind of late July blew through a caress of cypress trees lined up like a green wave in the cornfield. Looking west from a line of cypresses, the brook stretched out under a milky white sky, its poplars leaning over the sky-blue water which shimmered in the summer sun as if someone had tossed a million silver coins into it. In those days the world did not roll on a sea of bloodlust and war, but on a sea of grass and eternity. The sea did not dare assail us. Farmer and laborer were one. Us kids worked in that grass. Scared off the crows, chased away the stray goats, petted the lambs and scared them back toward common land. There was common land then: no lord of any manor dared think he owned the world.

I had been eating soft white cheese that afternoon in the haze of the afternoon and in my own sleep. The tart of pears and the black stain of walnuts and the blandness of the cheese shattered the heat and seeped into the canvas of my dreams. Under the sun we were all God's children, even the count, even Lydwina. God saw us all, saw Godelieve laying naked in the shallow pond where the reeds bobbed and the frogs croaked, saw the Bishop and Count Eustace and Lord Hemfrid and Lady Ogiva, saw Lambert the stable boy and Hacca the wine steward meeting in the dark of night to lay with one another on the straw in the barn, drunk on hippocras and unnatural lust, and saw that beautiful boy Lambert hanging from a tree above the brook, his perfectly shaped toes making ripples in the water, while a cloud of flies swarmed over his pallid yellow face, his stretched mouth, his yellowed teeth, his purple gums.

A milkmaid had been washing her pail in the stream when she found Lambert's body. She screamed. I sat up, rubbed the sleep out of my eyes, and ran to where she was. Everyone came running toward the brook, which lay on fallowing land outside of town.

'Pull him down gently, gently now,' one of the Count's men said. An old toothless farmer and his son gently lowered the body down from the tree. Lambert's body collapsed in a loose lump of yellowed limbs on the grassy bank of the brook.

'The devil is loose,' the farmer said, quietly.

By that time the bishop and his retinue had appeared behind the watch, which had arrived on the scene.

'You've informed Bertolf?' the Bishop said to the guard.

'I have, my lord,' replied the guard.

' "Be sober, be vigilant," or isn't that how the verse goes, my lord?' said a studious-looking monk in the Bishop's retinue. 'Something about a lion roaring in the wilderness?'

Sereno

'Now is not the time to spout verse,' the bishop replied, annoyed. 'Save your sermonizing for Sundays, my son.'

'The stable boy,' Frideswide said that evening at dinner. 'I just knew it. Never bring a boy like that too close, with that kind of face and body, do you hear me, girls? A lot trouble that boy was, from what I hear.'

'I just don't believe *why* he would kill himself like that. He seemed too stupid. What kind of trouble could he have possibly been in to begin with to warrant an end like that?' the laundry maid said.

'Stupid people kill themselves all the time,' Pieter said.

'I was speaking to *Editha*,' Frideswide said. 'Editha. Do you remember Richardis, the other laundry girl you worked with, who *mysteriously* disappeared from town last summer? My lord the Count had her *put away*, because,' she said, clearing her voice and lowering its tone, 'she was *in an interesting state.*'

'You don't say,' Editha replied, with a silly giggle. 'I thought her mother had died and she had to go bury her.'

'Oh that's what they *all* said,' Frideswide replied, responding with a silly giggle. 'And anyway, everyone said it was Lambert. They'd been out picking apples one day last September and I guess they must have... taken a tumble in the hay.'

'But now?'

'But now *what*? The rumor around town is that Lambert was up to no good. And I'm not one to gossip, so you didn't hear it from me, but...'

Frideswide rose and whispered something in Editha's ear. Editha turned pale and looked up at Frideswide, who gently nodded, as if she were relaying some very uncomfortable truth. Editha closed her eyes, drank from her cup of wine and smirked.

'You *must* be joking.'

'Would I lie?' Frideswide replied, wiping her hands on her apron.

Hacca was short and lean. His coat was of a burgundy color. His hair was clipped close to his head, and were he not Bertolf's wine steward, I would have thought him a monk. Very late in the evening, the night watch caught him trying to cross over to France with a bag full of crusty bread and some day-old chicken legs and a skin of weak summer wine. He'd stolen a mule from the count, but it was lame. He cursed God in the night for its hampering what would have been an escape.

But it was not Bertolf who had ordered him to be detained though. It was the Bishop. The Bishop's men had sat Hacca down in the hall on a low stool, and he was quivering with fright before the austere figure of that man of God.

'I want you to tell me about what you and Lambert were told to do,' he said. Before the both of them, the fire in the fireplace roared and snapped and popped, and from behind the safety of a tapestry, I saw Hacca look like he was staring into the mouth of hell.

'Me and Lambert were told to do nothing, sir,' he replied.

'Yes, you *were*,' the Bishop replied. 'The rumor is that you and Lambert and Bertolf were committing the sin of Sodom in the stables behind the manor house.'

Hacca's breathing became short and labored and panicky.

Saint Godelieve

'It's not true, my lord. You've been deceived.'

The Bishop laughed a hearty laugh and threw his cup of stale wine into the fire.

'Do you think I enjoy hearing rumor and gossip? Or am I to tarry among sinners all the days of my life? I came down to inquire about the death of the lady of the house, and here I am investigating a suicide.'

The Bishop walked over to Hacca and put his hand around Hacca's throat and squeezed tightly. 'Now you will tell me what you and Lambert did to Godelieve, and you will tell me *now*.'

He threw Hacca to the ground. Hacca coughed out a few sobs, caught his breath, reconciled himself with his fate.

'Bertolf had driven Godelieve away. You know that, right?'

'I do. Bertolf himself told me.'

A log on the fire snapped in two and collapsed into a pile of ashes and embers.

Hacca wrung his hands, swallowed hard. 'You must make sure no one knows about this.'

'He's a liar,' Bertolf said to the bishop. It was now Bertolf's turn to sit on the low stool before the Bishop. 'Anything Hacca tells you is probably a lie.'

'Then why'd you employ him as your wine steward?'

Bertolf hesitated for a minute.

'What does *that* have to do with Godelieve's death?'

'A great deal of trust is required for Hacca to serve your wine, my lord.'

Bertolf heaved a sigh of frustration and defeat.

'So I assume he's told you then.'

'He didn't tell me. I figured it out on my own.'

Bertolf shifted his gaze downward. The fire crackled in the fireplace. Even though it was summer, there was a cool, wet wind that blew in from the sea.

Saint Godelieve

'The cook told me you are accustomed to send up for wine in the third hour of the night. Rather late to be drinking, don't you think? You and Lambert were meeting each other at night. Hacca joined you. Godelieve must have seen you and Lambert together in the barnstable on the eve of St John.'

'I ought to cut his throat,' Bertolf said.

'I will have Hacca sent away to Bruges to answer for his crime. Lambert has paid for his. But you, my son—I am perplexed as to what will become of you.'

Bertolf let out a ragged breath. The truth was out.

The bishop gestured his men to bring Hacca into the room. They sat him down across from Bertolf. Bertolf went pale with fright.

'Speak, my son.'

'That day had been hot,' Hacca began. 'Too hot for any of us to remain in the house. I washed my face and hands in the stream. I found Lambert there. He'd gotten some ham and bread and a skin of hippocras from the kitchen. We walked back to the barnstable together. He had hung a lantern in the barn. The moon was rising, it was a little after sundown.'

'You were expecting the Count?'

'He always came out after nightfall. But that night had been different.'

'Why had it been different?'

'Because,' Hacca said, pausing. 'Because she saw us.'

'Who saw you?'

'The lady Godelieve, my lord.'

'We… were naked… together, all of us… drinking in the barn together. She had just happened to walk past us and we ran from her sight, but she still saw us. The Count… lost control of his reason, and ran after her half-dressed…'

'Then what happened?' the bishop asked.

One of the Bishop's men offered Hacca a cup of sour wine. Hacca drank the cup of wine with shaking hands, slowly, as if it were his last. 'When night had fallen he returned from the big house with instructions for us to get her to be quiet. She was always at the kitchen door, talking with the children. We thought she'd tell someone what she saw... her parents, maybe, or even your lordship.'

'Then what happened?'

'Lambert went up with a cudgel, and asked me to come and gag her. She was praying... together we took her bedsheet and wrapped around her neck. She didn't struggle. She was waiting for us. She screamed when Lambert started beating her and I put a pillow over her face. She stopped struggling after a few minutes.'

Hacca started to cry a plaintive cry, a child's cry in the voice of a man.

'She was innocent. I should have said no. She was so beautiful.'

'And so you took her body down to the mill pond and drowned her there.'

He nodded. The whole house was silent. Hacca wept, snivelled, laid out his sins for all to see.

'I wouldn't have done it if Bertolf had not told me and Lambert to go and do so. I thought that, if I did kill her, Bertolf would let me and Lambert leave to Bruges together. We had a pact to live in Bruges together.'

The Bishop rose and went to Hacca and placed his hand on his shoulder.

'I thank you, my son. Where you are going, my son, you shall have much time to think about the things you have done.'

That evening Editha and I shelled peas by the fire. Peter sat at the spit and turned a shank of lamb and some kidneys. Outside a cold, wet rain fell. It felt out of season, a chill touch of autumn in the warmth of summer.

'I wonder if she had prayed for them,' Editha said. 'As they killed her.'

'You believe all that drivel?' Pieter said, bewildered.

'If the Bishop says it's true, it's true.'

'I've heard that if you go out on St John's Eve, it's for mischief. Who's to say that Godelieve wasn't communing with the Devil out by the mill pond? Maybe she was courting the fairies. Maybe the fairies killed her by cursing her with death.'

'Oh but that's not all,' Frideswide said, coring an apple with her fingers.

'I always figured that Hacca was a little, you know, light in the loafers, if you know what I mean,' Editha replied.

'Oh come on!' Pieter replied. 'I'm not listening to this. All you women are all the same: gossip, gossip, gossip. And here you have a child sitting here listening to all of it. What a good example you're setting for him.'

'I saw Godelieve on St John's night too,' I replied. 'She brought us beans and bread. What she could not finish for dinner. And we all prayed to St John that night, for a good harvest.'

'Don't tell lies, child,' Pieter replied.

'I'm not telling any lies,' I said, fed up at last. I trembled with rage and grief. 'You can't tell me what to do and what to think. She was my friend. None of you liked her because she didn't fit in. They killed her because she was an outsider.'

I got up and balled up the apron I had wrapped around me and threw it on the table.

'Yes, she was praying for them,' I said. 'She prayed for *everyone*, including people who didn't deserve it.'

'Come and help me hang out the laundry, boy,' Frideswide said to me.

A meadow spotted with yellow flowers rolled out before us. We took the still-steaming wet clothes in a basket out toward a copse behind the house to dry.

'Lydwina's packing up to go to Bruges, I've been told,' Frideswide said. 'One of the Bishop's boys told me this morning. She and Bertolf have been placed "under interdict", whatever that means. But you didn't hear it from me. Maybe things might get a little easier for you, after all.'

'That'll never happen,' I said. 'She'll need someone to make sure the dog won't kill her cats. Or someone to turn out her slop bucket.'

Frideswide chuckled and pulled out a long white sheet and nodded to me to help her fold it. We stood out on the green grass and folded the white sheet together, before hanging it on a low branch to dry.

Saint Godelieve

'You best be careful with this,' Frideswide said. 'This is Godelieve's sheet.'

The white cloth sparkled in the sunlight. Frideswide always knew how to get white linen sheets very white.

I did not know then that I held the sheet Hacca and Lambert had used to strangle Godelieve and lower her body quietly into the murky dark of the mill-pond, swarming with flies and tadpoles and the vermin of the water. That sheet had pressed against her neck so tightly its fibers warped in strange places; that sheet was impregnated with thick wet air of the evening, had been saturated with the strange and ineffectual light of the moon, which drove men to madness, and which had inhaled all the foul exhalations of the world entire, had drawn to itself the evil of fairies and the greed of sprites that lurked in the trees, the same soul-stealing stuff that my mother had warned me to stay away from. How could evil be so close to me? How could I have held it in my hands? How could it sparkle so on this perfectly fresh summer morning?

No one will never know what I saw and felt—the caress of her brown hair, her wimple, her linen, dampened with water from the brook. I remember the rosy blush of her cheek, the mole that sat proudly on her upper lip, her Burgundian French that could never land in the low Belgian depths of the speech of the poor. Her low whispered prayer in church. The way her hand clasped mine when we went to scare off crows together.

Her smile. Her eyes. Her hands.

I wanted to jump in the grave with her, become living earth, commingle my living flesh with her dead flesh, become one earth together.

When she was taken from us, we all looked to that same silent God who existed behind the fixed stars, and asked Him why. God responded in the sighs of the breeze, in letters from the Pope that we couldn't read, in the words of the Mass only a few of us knew.

Saint Godelieve, we said, *pray for us*. But unlike those heroes who stared at us from faded paintings on the chapel wall Godelieve had been alive, had not emerged from the hissing entrails of a dragon or ferried by angels to mountains where only the frenzied heathen danced, where Jews had spoken to God. She had prayed for me. Had spoken my name.

Saint Godelieve, I said, *pray for me, a poor sinner.*

Saint Godelieve

I loved her, you see. I searched her eyes like I had searched out the skies for signs, warnings; I had searched every line in her irises, onto which God Himself had written His name. Even in the dark of her eyes closed in death I saw the Milky Way, an entire field full of summer stars as bright as sackcloth into which a thousand tiny diamonds had been scattered. She had pointed out which stars formed constellations with me as we sat under a huge oak tree one evening, and guiding my hand, she pointed out the Lion, the Virgin, the Winged Horse, St John the Baptist's head on the silver dish of the Moon, his face a mass of thorns and stone.

Sereno

Colonial Revival

THROUGHOUT THE SIXTY-SEVEN YEARS of her life, no one could have said that Alice Debrett was an easy player. No one could have accused her of being lazy. She had been the first to go to college in her family. It made her Marine father proud. She had been the first to leave Spokane to study medicine in California and had done so well that within the first year of her residency she had already managed to find a husband and find a good job. Rather than just go back to Washington to practice medicine there, however, she instead stayed in Portland to start working as an obstetrician. And it was at St Vincent's that she had proven herself a capable and cool-headed deliverer of babies.

But even with the gift of patience, she couldn't abide certain circumstances. Certain people. She cringed when heard the sound of flip-flops on hospital floors. She dreaded the sight of spaghetti strap chemises, athlesiure wear, yoga pants. She held in her breath when she saw the dark-skinned janitor pass by in his coveralls with his yellow mop bucket. She avoided taking buses if she had to get somewhere close in. She did not greet the cashiers at the Safeway on Hawthorne or on Weidler, because she did not know if they could speak English well or not. She had instinctively learned to not give money to the homeless, to not speak to Black men on the Max, to avoid large crowds of people who spoke Spanish on trips to the Saturday market. When she shopped for her favorite dark turtleneck sweaters at Fred Meyer—so necessary on those gloomy days of early spring—she wore big dark sunglasses and clutched her purse close to her.

No one else could be blamed for these presumptions. After all, Portland was a big town with unfamiliar people. Eastmoreland did not resemble anything like what it did twenty or thirty years ago. And every year, another old friend died or moved away, and the circle of unfamiliar people and situations closed in on her.

Then one autumn, her husband Phill died in the arms of a woman he'd met at a business conference in Reno. The other woman was much younger, a poodle-haired redhead with a banking job, someone she'd been sure Phill had invited to their annual Christmas party. And so it was then, upon closing the casket lid and retrieving the calla lilies from the funeral home, that she had abruptly turned off a natural trust in the goodness and innocence in people.

Colonial Revival

So naturally it seemed suspicious when Alice saw that a Mexican man was moving into Margaret Shapiro's rather new house across the street. She sent emails to the HOA and inquired whether subletting a room in this part of Eastmoreland was legal. The reply from Jack Hornby, the head of the HOA, was that Margaret Shapiro was in her rights to allow folks to live in her mother-in-law. Something about the mother-in-law irked Alice Debrett. She remembered the ruckus that accompanied the construction of the Neoclassical Revival-style 'poolhouse' ADU, with its French doors that Alice was sure did not match neither Margaret Shapiro's back door, to say nothing of the front. Such architectural omissions were glaring and unforgivable in a neighborhood like Eastmoreland. People in the neighborhood relied on architectural order, a hypostatic union of identity and meaning in this neighborhood.

She phoned her next door neighbor, Louise Morris.

'Are you sure he's not part of the landscaping crew?' Dr Debrett asked, parting the sheer curtain in her living room and looking out on them.

'I don't know,' Louise said. She was a plump, silly little woman who wore a lot of yellow. 'Have you spoken with Margie?'

'No,' Dr Debrett said. 'You know, it's been about two years since we spoke. She came over when Phill died. She brought over a bread pudding.'

'Oh really, now? I never got to try some. I wish we hadn't been on vacation when all that went down. I keep on hearing her bread pudding is so good. What does it taste like?'

Debrett paused to remember this salient fact. 'Come to think of it, Louise, I can't remember at all what it tasted like. I know it had raisins.'

Alice sat back in her recliner and heaved a sigh.

'Maybe I'm just overthinking this, Louise. Maybe he's a nice guy. Maybe they're working for Margie. Maybe something happened.'

'You might want to ask her,' Louise replied. 'Say. I was going to ask you. Do you think we'll get invited to Trudy Valence's 4th of July barbecue again this year? I saw her at church. She said she wasn't thinking of giving one. Something about the caterer not being able to come back from Singapore and all that. And you know how things have been with her husband's broken hip.'

Colonial Revival

Alice Debrett watched the young, handsome man load a last few boxes onto a dolly and wheel it, walking backward, into the black rectangle of Margie's front door. The door closed softly, soundlessly; the street was peaceful once more.

Alice Debrett put on a blush angora turtleneck and a pair of lavender pants and ran a comb through her bob cut and went to speak with Margaret Shapiro. Margie had been for years the kind of woman that Alice had wanted to have a strong cup of tea with. They'd seen one another in town—at the New Seasons or at a boutique, invariably. Margie did not choose to have children with her late husband Frank, and had been wise enough to avoid the intrigues of neighborhood mothers. Instead, she hoarded old watercolors of wisterias, wore costume jewelry, and read books she'd seen reviewed on C-Span.

Margie had been waiting for Alice at the door. Margaret Shapiro had a fine, onyx-like quality to her. Refined, polished, with a nearly all-black wardrobe. Alice knew that Margie taught sociology at Reed and Frank had taught history.

'Do you mind telling me who those people moving into your new mother-in-law are?' Alice said.

Margie smiled, anticipating the tension that came with a question like this.

'One of my graduate students, Alice. By the way, nice to see you. It's been about two years. We rarely get to speak anymore; it's a shame, don't you think?'

'It is,' Alice said, with a tone of regret. 'I couldn't help but notice from my living room. I thought, it must seem rather odd for someone to just start moving furniture on Saturday morning—'

'I don't think anyone has a problem with that.'

'Oh, you don't think so?' she replied, a little bemused. 'Not even Jack?'

'Oh, Jack's easy,' Margie replied waving off the comment with a hand. 'It's all kismet, I'm sure. We're not making a scene, are we?'

'Well, no...' Alice replied.

'Then I'm sure it'll be OK. Why don't you get acquainted with him?' She leaned out of the door and cupped her hand toward the dark-skinned man wiggling a table off of his beat-up pickup truck. 'Juan! Come and meet a neighbor.'

Colonial Revival

The hair rose on the back of Alice's neck. Meeting the handsome man? In the middle of the street? With his dirty hands, his sweaty brow? He ascended the winding paved steps up to Margie's front door and took off a rough leather work glove.

'Alice, Juan Mendez. Juan, this is Alice Debrett, she's our across-the-street neighbor.'

Alice sized Juan up. He was thin, handsome with a neatly shaved little black mustache and gauged ears, a spiky haircut. He looked like the many fathers she'd delivered babies for over the years; all of them, she guessed, incapable of speaking English. But this one was Americanized. He looked American, groomed and coiffed like one of the boys she'd seen frequent the aisles of the vegan grocery she occasionally went to.

'It's a pleasure,' Juan said, putting a hand out. She gingerly shook it and quickly picked a handkerchief and wiped her hand with it.

'I've been told you're a graduate student under Dr Shapiro,' Alice said.

'That's correct,' Juan said, not looking at Alice wiping her hand with the handkerchief. He smiled intently at her, determined to look her straight in the eye. 'I'm working on getting my PhD in housing and community development. She's a great teacher, don't you think?'

Margie blushed and let out an embarrassed gasp. 'I am sure you're being very generous Juan.'

There was no unaccented English in his speech. Yes, he was Americanized, maybe even a citizen.

'Where are you originally from, if you don't mind me asking?' Alice said. 'It's very interesting seeing… new faces show up in Eastmoreland. You've got the whole neighborhood talking, you know.'

'That's not necessarily true, Alice,' Margie said with a nervous twinge in her voice. 'I haven't heard anything at all. Not a peep from Jack in the HOA. Let's all… come in for tea, shall we?'

'I'm from here,' Juan replied. 'I'm from Portland, like you.'

'Oh, I'm not from *Portland*,' Alice replied. 'I was born in Spokane. But I've lived here for years. And so has Margie.'

Juan's smile faded a little as he apprehended Alice's angle.

'I should get back to moving. I'm sorry. Such a pleasure getting to know you, Dr Debrett.'

Margie Shapiro gave Alice a self-satisfied look.

'He's got a few things left to move in,' she said. 'I vetted him, Alice. I'd really like to keep affairs in my house just to me, if you don't mind.'

'I don't mind at all, actually,' Alice said, coolly. 'I just happened to be curious, is all.'

But something about Juan did bother her. The way he looked at her, the way his hand had gripped hers with such concrete intent. Did he really have to shake someone's hand like that? The things he brought with him were rain-spattered hand-me-downs. Old furniture, things that no one wanted anymore. Alice retreated back into her house and called Jack Hornby, and asked him to convene an HOA meeting.

'I think you're being really very silly about this,' Jack Hornby said. 'Alice. Listen to me. I have chili to make and grandkids to visit. Can this wait?'

Sereno

'I don't think it can. You see, I don't know him. And if I don't know him, I'm not comfortable with him.'

Jack Hornby let out an audible sigh. 'Alice, honey, you don't have to *know* him. Are we done here?'

Over the next few months, it became apparent to everyone on Alice's street that Juan was just a normal, quiet person, another Portlander who didn't have a house of their own and was OK with having to make do in someone else's house. He sometimes rode his bike home on the warm, sunny days or else just walked down the hill toward the bus station. Alice watched him from her veranda, watched him until his smooth lean brown frame turned the corner and disappeared behind the flowering privet hedge that demarcated the end of the street. Sometimes he drove Margie up to Safeway to get groceries in her car, and the two could be heard laughing to one another as they moved their groceries into the house.

But then the Fourth of July came, and Alice waited for an invitation to arrive in the mailbox. It was a tradition for Margie Shapiro to invite some neighborhood friends to her annual Fourth of July picnic. Alice always went through the trouble to prepare a sugar-free Jello Pie for the Shapiros. Sometimes Phill came, if he felt like it. But this year, the handsome dark-skinned stranger drove off with Margie in the passenger seat of her car. Trudy Valence's husband Tom had a hip replacement and there was no Fourth of July barbecue at her house, either.

'It's really quite strange, don't you think?' she said to Louise that evening. 'They could have gone anywhere, I mean. She always has her party tonight.'

Down the street a few neighborhood children lit fireworks and squealed as a shower of silver sparks spurted into the heavy night air.

'Alice, honey—give her a break. She's sixty-six. Now that Frank's dead, there's no way she can put on a party like that. You've had it out for this guy ever since he moved here.'

'I have *not*, Louise. I'm *not* a prejudiced person. But it all seems very strange to me. To have him living there. You know, he may not even be paying rent. How do you think she keeps that house clean?'

'Maybe she has his mother come over and clean it when we're not looking,' Louise said with a chortle. 'You know, that's probably what she did.'

Alice laughed a little and sipped her solitary glass of white wine, turned down the TV a little.

'We didn't have Mexicans in Spokane,' she said. 'Or rather, we did, but they stayed on their side of the tracks.'

'Mmm-hmm,' Louise replied. 'Is that where that comes from, then.'

'Like I said,' Alice said, as if she were putting up all her bets for good. 'We didn't talk to them, and to now have them talking to us all feels very strange.'

'You'll never *guess* who made a blueberry cobbler for the book club this year,' Louise Morris then said.

To break the ice one summer evening, Margaret Shapiro brought the young man onto Alice's veranda. Alice demurely opened up her door and peeked outside.

'Come out and play mahjong with us, Alice. Juan's made some tacos. He wants to meet you. He's very interested in your work at St Vincent's. What do you say?'

This trespass was a bare-faced insult to her. The Shapiros had never, in all their nearly forty years of living on her street, even dared to step foot on her lawn. When the Shapiros walked their ancient Bichon Frise down the street they had purposefully avoided Alice's terrace of portulaca and lava rocks. And now, to have this stranger with this old Jew woman inviting her out for daiquiris and mahjong!

'I really don't know,' Alice replied. 'Do you know how to play mahjong, Juan?'

Juan beamed and nodded. 'Dr Shapiro's showed me a couple of times.'

'But you'll never beat me. What do you say, Alice? Come out.'

Alice reluctantly accepted their invitation. Juan led her to the back of Margie's lot and showed them the table where he had served dinner.

Frank had laid out the backyard to be amenable to these parties: there was a hammock and hostas and a rose bower full of fat French hybrids and the pool-house with its French doors was very pretty indeed. Alice felt small in this immensely shaded backyard, with the pool invitingly blue and the massive elm covering it all with a sort of arboreal supremacy she'd only seen in magazines.

To add insult to injury, Louise Morris was there with Jack Hornby. The Mexican had laid out a tray of tacos—soft-style, the way that Phill liked them—and made guacamole and salsa. And to Alice's surprise, the old Jew woman loved his tacos, savored them, raved about them.

'Just so you know, he's not my houseboy,' Margie Shapiro said, pouring a daiquiri for Alice. 'He's a brilliant scholar.'

'Where'd you go to school, Juan?'

'PSU,' Juan replied. 'I did my undergrad in urban planning.'

'Oh, isn't that something?' Louise replied. 'You're not planning to tear up any houses around here, are you?'

'Oh no,' Juan replied, sitting down. He folded his long fingers and looked at his row of mahjong tiles.

'Two dot,' he said. 'No, I'm interested in making neighborhoods, not destroying them. In fact, I love historic preservation.'

Colonial Revival

'Alice's husband used to make subdivisions. Back when you were on a cloud. Tell him what Phill did,' Louise said.

Alice heaved an uncomfortable sigh. 'Well, if you have to know. He was very active in neighborhood planning. Historic properties, as well. He didn't do any of the actual planning, though. He just got the money together to build houses in Gresham and Beaverton. Chances are you've probably lived in one of his apartments.'

'Actually,' Juan replied not taking his eyes off the tiles, 'I grew up off of 52nd and Holgate. Just a normal frame house. Nothing too fancy.'

As the evening wore on the white rum coursed through Alice's gullet and settled, like poison, in her stomach. Juan was indeed very charming: he made jokes, told anecdotes, made everyone feel very loosened up. Only Frank could have matched that sort of freewheeling air.

He went back into the house and brought out a dessert: a shaky pan of tricolor Jello squares stuck through with bits of fruit and topped with chiffonesque ripples of whipped cream. He served this in small Fiestaware plates and passed around another pitcher of strawberry daiquiri.

'Would you be interested in talking to me, Dr Debrett?' he said. 'I think having your opinion on maternal healthcare in developing urban communities would be super essential for the work I'm doing now.'

Alice gave Juan a look over.

This Mexican, with his interests in making community, she thought. With his fruity Jello salads and his big pitcher of daiquiri mix, his red-stained fingers. He had gone through so much trouble to come off as smarter than he actually was. To shrug off Phill's efforts to bring his people out of the gutter where they languished, picking melons and slicing through cabbage. To presume that he could simply address her that way.

'I really don't have anything to add to the conversation,' she replied. 'But I'm sure there's enough literature on the subject—maybe Dr Shapiro can point you in the right direction.'

'Oh, I think my own experiences are pretty out-of-date. Juan's efforts are for the future. You've always been the youngest of our little home group, Alice. I've always admired that you've had your head on straight. And your house is so beautiful. Wouldn't it be nice to visit for a bit just to chat?'

'It *is* a beautiful house,' Juan replied. 'Mission Revival style?'

'*Spanish colonial revival*,' she said with an incisiveness in her tone. 'There are regional variations. They're very distinct styles. We don't have the crossbeams.'

'*Vigas*. Ah, yes, I see now.'

'What did you say?'

'*Vigas*,' Juan said, putting a tile down. 'That's what they're called. I saw them in New Mexico.'

'Is your family from there, Juan? Seems like a long way away from home for you.' Jack Hornby said.

Juan looked up and took a sip from his daiquiri.

'I was born in Portland, it's home to me. I was only in New Mexico to teach elementary school a year after I graduated.'

Alice swallowed her disgust with them all. Above their table the bug light zapped an errant cranefly and it drifted to the ground with the gravity of a falling leaf.

It was apparent now that Alice had seen for herself that Juan had been helping Margie to get work done around the house. Margie had shown off how thorough Juan was. He swept the floors, dusted off the piano, polished the banisters, stoked the fireplace, and of course, had prepared the cocktails. Margie never had the sense to hire a maid, Alice figured. It would have done her some good. But Margie had always been very good as a housekeeper. Juan was just playing catch-up. It was not his own furniture which he had moved into the mother-in-law he lived in, she found out. It had been some of Margie's old furniture, packed away in storage for years. So the upstart brown skinned wanderer who claimed to have been born and raised in Portland had no assets of his own. No car, no furniture. Most likely no money. Alice recalled what her father had said of Mexicans. Parasites, all of them, living off the skids and only content to occupy places where they were not welcome. It all became clear that Juan was nothing more than Margie's caretaker.

The poor old Jew woman. Soon death would come for her like it had come for poor old Frank and the both of them would be sleeping under the sod at Lone Fir near the McLoughlin graves that Frank had been so keen on preserving. And then what might happen? To leave the house to Juan? What did *he* know about life in Eastmoreland?

Colonial Revival

On certain late evenings, Alice would stare out from her bedroom window and watch the silhouettes dance across the beige curtains in Margie's room across the street. For years Frank had a certain routine after work—the light from the TV would flicker in their living room until precisely 9:30 PM, when Frank would move to his studio directly above the living room. The light would stay on there until 11 PM, when he would light the low lamp in their master bedroom. And then he would sleep. Alice had timed the intervals of lights going on, lights going off, like the contractions of a woman about to give birth. But Juan had disrupted all of this. He left lights on, turned lights off at odd intervals. Sometimes she heard the splash of pool water at 1 AM and imagined his naked brown body gliding under the pool lights there in the dark of Margie Shapiro's backyard. He could have brought a girlfriend over, Alice thought to herself. He'd fuck her on the deck. In the deck chair that she had sat in during that party, or in the papasan chair that Jack Hornby sat in like the miserable old bump on a log that he was.

She crushed paper Dixie cups in her hands thinking of his naked body, the warmth of it as it would slip effortlessly in the clear blue water of Frank Shapiro's pool. She imagined Margie's sad blue eyes watching him, sipping her afternoon Manhattan, trading anecdotes with him about how her mother had sang in Marc Blitzstein musicals in the '30s and how her father defended longshoremen.

The next day Alice drove to Safeway and bought a daffodil cake mix. She asked Louise to use her stand mixer, and over tea the women decided to take the cake to Margie's and say hello.

The two of them walked side-by-side up the steps to Margie's house. Dr Shapiro answered the door. As always, she had on a tidy black frock and tiny black velour slippers.

'A daffodil cake?' Margie Shapiro said. 'I simply don't know *what* to say.'

'Oh you know, I just see you out alone in front of the house. With that young man. I saw you planting new flowers.'

'Really girls, this is too much. What *is* this all about?'

Colonial Revival

'You can never be too sure,' Alice replied. 'Gardening? At your age? Don't you think that's sort of excessive?'

'Really, Alice. You can be very rude when you're trying to be nice,' Margie said, seeing right through the doctor's ruse. 'If you just want to come inside just say so. We're all friends here.'

There was not a speck of dust in Margaret Shapiro's house. In the foyer their marriage portrait glistened from behind the matte of a glass and silver frame. Frank and Margie were always the moderns, never content to keep up with the Joneses as they were the Joneses everyone spoke of. She always had singularly white, freshly clipped calla lilies in the terrazzo vases in her house. Margie had idolized weird old Frank Shapiro, his ancient coins and his collection of Roman glass shards, his bald head with its remaining strands of dark hair, his hunched and speckled neck. The house was still carpeted as it had been during the mid-nineties in that same drab grey that had been once the only viable option among the wealthy in Portland. The chandeliers were still made of amber glass; the foyer table a glaringly dated combination of bronze pasta tubes and oblong glass.

She found Juan shirtless, polishing the silver.

Louise tried to hold in a gasp but it came out as a giggle.

Dr Shapiro took off her glasses and rubbed her eyebrows.

'Busy at work on your dissertation, I see?' Alice said.

'Part of the deal is that I help Dr Shapiro with daily tasks. We have a dinner party on Saturday.'

'A dinner party? You realize most of the people in this neighborhood are on vacation, right?' Alice said.

'Not for you all,' Dr Shapiro said. 'For Juan's friends from school.'

'How do you think you're going to manage parking for that, Margie?'

'I should get going,' Louise said, her curiosity sated. 'I'll call you, Alice.'

Margaret sat down and looked up at Alice's pristine offering, her black turtleneck, her long silver chain with its ball at the end.

'Like we've managed dinner parties for years, Dr Debrett. I emailed Jack. I assume you've been going to the HOA meetings.'

'I wasn't aware of any meeting,' Alice replied.

The front door closed and Alice suddenly felt how oppressive this old Jew woman and her Mexican lackey polishing silver he could never afford could be.

'Either way,' Margie said, sighing. 'We'll be quiet as we can. Just seven friends, is all. His friends. You know, the late Dr Shapiro did the same thing with his history students every year. Every *year*, Alice.'

'So then how do I know they'll be Reed students, too?'

'You won't,' Juan replied, finally. He looked up at her with the sort of defiance she had only seen from the Filipino nurses who had dared defy her orders. Those nurses never lasted under her.

'You won't know and it won't involve you. Is that OK with you? Or do you need it all on paper?"

'Listen, young man. Unless you start paying taxes, like I do, and making a concerted effort to actually include yourself in your community, rather than writing about it for a grade, you have no reason to assume that anyone of us in this neighborhood will tolerate seven people doing all sorts of things in one of our houses.'

Dr Shapiro rose sharply. 'I think you should apologize.'

He gently laid a hand on her forearm.

'I'm articulate enough to speak for myself,' Juan replied, calmly. 'OK, Dr Debrett. I get that you're not comfortable with me living in Eastmoreland. I could tell that you were a little uncomfortable at our last little get-together. You heard it from Dr Shapiro herself: there have been get-togethers before and everyone was fine with it.'

'Listen,' she said, channelling her father. 'All I'm saying is, I *don't* know what kind of person you are.'

'And why should he have to explain himself to you, Alice?' Dr Shapiro said.

Alice couldn't answer that. The rage now vibrated inside her thin frame. For a moment she thought of throwing the daffodil cake into his face.

'I don't know what you are or where you come from, Juan,' Alice said, taking a deep breath. 'Gosh, I *hate* having these conversations. I'm sure you think I'm a racist or something.'

'Yes, I do,' Juan replied. 'Yes, Dr Debrett. I *do* think you're a racist.' He looked back at Margie. 'I was expecting this. You were right.'

'Thank you for the cake, Alice. I think you should go, my dear.'

'Bet you weren't expecting me to call your bluff, right?'

Margie's voice grew sharp. 'Juan. That's *enough*.'

'No,' Alice said, gritting her teeth. 'You're wrong. I'm *not* a racist.'

Juan stood up and pulled on his Hawaiian shirt. 'I sent the email to Jack. In fact I invited him. And if you want to go, sure. Why not. I'm not a racist, either, Alice. I'm not looking to making any enemies here.'

Sereno

After Dr Shapiro had gently tugged her out of her house she immediately went back to her house and called Louise.

'You won't believe what he assumes about me.'

'What's that?' Louise cooed into the phone. 'Hold on! Let me turn down the TV thingy the kids installed.'

She waited while Louise fumbled with her TV. She breathlessly returned to the phone. 'OK, tell me.'

'He thinks... I'm a... *racist*, Louise.' By then the anger had subsided and she saw recognized herself as a busybody, a fool alone in her house of low lights and neutral textures. 'To think of me as a racist. Can you beat that?'

'Well, I don't know,' Louise said. '*Are* you?'

'No, Louise. No. I am *not* a racist. But the fact that he thinks that about me. *He's* the racist one.'

'I think you should tell people on Facebook, you know. I'm sure other people might agree.'

'I don't do those sort of things, Louise.'

Louise spooned a forkful of lemon meringue pie into her mouth.

'I think you're just being very unfair, Louise went on, her mouth full. 'I mean, he seems like such a nice young man. To make the effort of taking care of Margie like that. Wouldn't your son do the same for you?'

She hadn't thought of Skippy for months until then. Like her father, Skip had left home to be Marine and now lived, anonymously, in Connecticut with a woman Alice barely knew and children she rarely saw. Alice only summoned them when it was appropriate— Thanksgiving and Christmas—and their relationship had been more or less cool and off-handed. But she had hoped that, like Juan, Skippy might one day care for her in her frailty. The house was her only companion, and the things she had bought over the span of four decades had replaced husband and children.

She emailed Jack Hornby that night with the subject in big bold letters: URGENT. HOUSE PARTY AT SHAPIRO RESIDENCE. She gave a few identifiable details. Jack wrote back before one o'clock with a terse reply that it was, in fact, not against HOA rules to have parties of more than five people in one residence at one time. Jack said that other people in the neighborhood did not feel uncomfortable with Juan's bike riding up and down the street twice a day, despite old Trudy Valence at the end of the block calling the non-emergency lines to complain about his early and late comings and goings. Alice took a shower and let the weight of Jack's decision fall on her like a gentle rain.

A defiant calm settled on her: she was right, had always been. Nobody, in fact, had wanted this dirty Mexican living in Eastmoreland.

But direct opinions were in short supply at the actual HOA meeting. Of course Dr Shapiro had decided not to show up, furthering the rift. Trudy Valence had just wanted to know who the young man was and why he had even bothered to sweep up the broken Scotch broom blossoms that littered her driveway. Alice had even vainly thought that Jack would somehow spring to her defense. He had managed to admit, in his usual spineless way, that since the party hadn't actually taken place, there was no way to determine if an infraction was about to take place. 'For example,' Jack said, 'Five people could show up. Or four.' Finally he put the email on the table and looked at Alice. 'Or no one.'

'Don't you think you're being childish? Alice, this is very uncharacteristic of you. You're a doctor, for god sakes. I would have expected you to have a little more humanity than what I am hearing now. We know this guy. So what if he has a couple of his buddies over? He's not the kind of guy that gives me the heebie-jeebies, Alice. I don't think he's gonna be starting a cartel war on the block.'

'But the rule is that you can't have more than five people in a house. The parking situation is what gets me, Jack. It's the parking that I'm worried about.'

'Why don't you just say what you're thinking for all of us, Alice?'

'Say what?' Alice replied.

'I mean, why don't you just tell me and everyone else here what you think about Juan. That you don't like him because he doesn't look like all the other folks here.'

Never before had such a mortifyingly thick silence impregnated this modest, nondescript corner of the library before.

Jack Hornby took off his glasses and pointed a fat index finger at Alice.

'If you're wastin' my time to somehow complain about this Mexican guy being in Margie's house, you got another thing coming. Where I grew up in Hillsboro we made peace with those folks. They came up here every year to pick berries at my dad's farm and I never gave 'em any trouble. Don't do what I know you're wanting to do, Alice. It's not worth it.' He slammed the HOA binder shut.

'Now get the hell outta here, Alice. Meeting's adjourned.'

In early September, Dr Shapiro hired a caterer and a florist. They came in white vans and brought out two long tables. The landscaper came one Friday morning to trim the boxwoods and water the dahlias. The caterer took out a large box of white lanterns and began hanging them from the portico of Dr Shapiro's entryway. Alice watched them all from her own veranda, writing down their times of arrival and departure. She had done something she had once vowed to never do: she walked down to the Plaid Pantry and bought a pack of American Spirits and sat on the veranda and smoked every last one until she had crumpled the pack in her and brushed the loose tobacco leaves onto her boxwoods. On Saturday morning the caterer came again—a ragtag group of short men and women in ill-fitting clothing—and Dr Shapiro came out of her house, greeted them on the threshold, and then walked across the street to Louise's house, and then to Jack's house, and then to Trudy's house at the end of the street. She walked back up the hill, and for a moment Alice had hoped the old woman would grovel at her feet, but such a vindication would never come. Dr Shapiro simply went back into her house.

At seven, the neighbors began to peer out of their curtains to see the inexorable line of cars that would assemble themselves up and down the street. Instead they all saw two carloads of people, one ferried by an Uber and the other by a Lyft driver. The group stepped out quietly onto Dr Shapiro's walkway. Alice heard one of them exclaim 'wow' before they all went into Dr Shapiro's house in a single file. The door clicked shut and nothing else was heard.

She sat there on the veranda until it was very late, contemplating Juan's invitation. She imagined the kind of food Margie had ordered. She always used the same caterer and the same appetizers, rumaki, bruschetta with olive tapenade, chili sauce meatballs, baklava... it was all the same.

She heard a few brief, bright laughs from Margie's backyard. She tried to fish out of the dark air snatches of conversation. They could be talking about anything, she thought. They could be talking about Margie, about the neighborhood. Stupid people, all of them. They'd never have the neighborhood she'd had, they could work and they'd never come close to what she and Phill had had. Stupid, selfish, hard-headed people, all of them.

Then Juan came out of the front door for a smoke break with a friend. Both men stood under the light and puffed away for thirty minutes, carrying on a conversation that she couldn't understand. Alice flicked on the porch lights twice as if to shoo them back inside. Finally, she opened the door and came out on the veranda with her cell phone, sat in the wicker rocking chair, and stared them down.

'The neighbors,' she heard Juan say, with a chuckle. They tossed their cigarettes into the street and walked back inside.

Pigs, all of them, Alice thought. She dashed off a note on Nextdoor and took a picture of the house. THIS IS NOT THE WAY TO HAVE A PARTY IN EASTMORELAND, the text post read.

At 2 AM the party definitively ended and the same group of seven people waited apprehensively outside for their Ubers home to show up. Juan was a little tipsy and a little loud, and gathered them all under the portico for a photograph. She heard them all say goodbye, heard them all slam the car doors shut, heard the Uber back up into her driveway, and drive away. Alice sat at her laptop desk in the master bedroom, writing down the times of every loud noise she heard. A neat, angry little list of numbers ran down in a vertical line on a legal pad.

She thought of putting it all up on Facebook and letting Eastmoreland deal with Margie Shapiro. Even Jack Hornby had failed her now, and he was the man in charge of the HOA. If Phill were still alive, he'd go right down to Margie Shapiro's and yell her ear off, tell that Mexican what for, tell him to get the hell on back to Gresham or Fairview where he really came from. *Put it all up on Facebook, let the neighborhood deal with it,* Louise had said. *Just wash your hands of it.*

When sleep finally came to her it was almost four-thirty. She slept until ten, then showered, breakfasted and put on a pair of blush twill pants and a deep fuschia sweater. She crossed the street and knocked on Margie Shapiro's door.

'I don't want to talk to you,' Margie replied.

'Do you know what time I got to sleep? Four in the morning.'

'Really, Alice, you are so crass to come over here to complain.'

'I counted eleven people in your house last night. Eleven. And I heard you until 2 AM making all sorts of noise.'

Alice's face was beginning to twist up as the rage began rising in her. Margie held on the to jamb of her front door.

'I couldn't sleep *at all*, Margaret. It's unacceptable.'

Dr Shapiro closed the door to the house and stepped out onto the portico.

'I don't know who you *are* anymore, Alice. You know, I must have been really mistaken thinking you were some great doctor. The truth is you're a horrible human being. You have been since Phill died.'

'Shut up,' Alice said, balling up her fists. 'Phill has *nothing* to do with this.'

'I feel sorry for you. How empty your life is. You and me have all the money in the world, and when someone like Juan shows up, you just can't stand it. You can't stand sharing anything with anyone. Look at you. Look at how ridiculous you look right now. Shaking the way you are. Very empty.'

Alice closed her eyes and sighed deeply, tried hard to avoid slapping Margie.

'Listen to me, Dr Shapiro. I'm going to warn you. There'll be trouble if this goes on. With the HOA and with me.'

Margie Shapiro laughed. 'Another empty threat from the Dr. Alice Debrett. What's next, you're going to start counting the inches between the trash cans? Just stop, Alice. You're really very pathetic.'

Something shattered inside Alice. She smashed a fist into the side of Margie's face. She pulled the collar of Margie's blouse, swung her around, and pushed her down the stone steps. Margie rolled down and landed face-first against the lava rock border where the landscaper had laid down fresh mulch.

Juan opened the door. His first sight was Alice's balled up fists, her blonde bob, her pink sweater, the ugly shoes she wore. He caught sight of Margie laying on the ground, unresponsive, blood trailing from a gash on her forehead.

He rushed to her.

Alice looked at her hands, gathered herself, and let loose a relaxed sigh.

'I'm calling the police.'

'No,' Juan replied. I'll call them. You pushed her.'

'You have no way of proving that,' Alice replied, coolly. 'It's my word against yours.'

'You did this,' Juan replied. 'You racist bitch. I knew it.'

'Don't talk to me, wetback.' She put on a pair of sunglasses. 'The cops'll be here soon enough; I'd start getting your stories straight.'

She said nothing more, crossed the street and went back into her house. She went to the kitchen and called Louise first.

She watched Juan crouch low and quickly call the paramedics. He struggled to keep up with the 911 call, he had to repeat himself over and over again.

Colonial Revival

Alice had perched herself at her desk upstairs. She undid the jalousie and stared down at the scene unfolding below before her.

'I was just at Margie's and you'll never guess what just happened,' Alice said, taking off her sunglasses. 'That Mexican boy just pushed Margie down the steps. And now she's bleeding from a gash on her forehead.'

'No! You're *kidding.*'

'I am not. She's got a contusion on her head and he's trying to get her inside the house.'

Alice watched Louise run out of her house and towards Margie's house.

'Don't you go anywhere, Juan! The police are on their way. Good Lord, I knew something like this was going to happen.'

She watched Louise run back into her house.

'I've got to let you go, Alice. I need to call the police.'

Alice poured herself a glass of iced tea. She went downstairs, emerged magisterially on her veranda, and watched the police cruisers arrive from the comfort of her wicker rocking chair. There were four of them, with an ambulance and a fire truck in tow. Alice watched as the police assess the location, set up a perimeter, call for backup. A few moments later, they'd tackled Juan to the ground, tased him, and pushed him into the back of a cruiser.

Alice spent a few moments constructing the story she would tell the police. The policeman would believe her; there were no other witnesses than she. They would believe her over Juan any day.

She had anticipated the sight of the young, muscled policeman ascending the steps to her veranda to knock on her door. They always sent the young ones to do the dirty work, talk to the witnesses, take down statements. She ran a brush through her hair and pinched her cheeks in the mirror.

'I saw the whole thing and can tell you exactly what happened,' Alice said to the young officer at the door. 'Would you like to come in?'

Colonial Revival

Sereno

Breathless

ON A WET, DISMAL EVENING UNDER THE awning at Whole Foods one November, Anthony nervously checked his phone and watched the number 8 bus arrive at the intersection.

'I'm sorry, just give me 2 mins,' Josh texted. 'So many people.'

Of course the bus was late, and Josh had been late getting off of work.

The rain had flooded the streets and clogged the sewers with fallen leaves, and the bus's windshield wipers sloshed back and forth in six o'clock traffic. Josh was reticent about meeting Anthony. Anthony didn't look real, didn't sound real; you couldn't just say you were 'an artist & writer' in Portland without looking like either a liar or a dipshit. Besides, there were three other dudes waiting in line: Andrew the waiter, Alex the barista, Eduardo the taco truck cook, Rhys the English graphic designer. All of these boys had vied for Josh's attention during the year but he had all turned them down. And now Mother Nature seemed to be warning him that this evening would be preternaturally ill-fated.

Sereno

'Josh!" Anthony said, holding a copy of the *Mercury* over his head. 'You're a lot taller in person, you know that?'

Josh smiled. 'Hey. Yeah, I'm sorry I was late. Traffic, you know. It's terrible.'

'Yeah, tell me about it! But you're OK, right?'

'I mean, I'm alive,' Josh replied, walking his bike to the corner of the block. 'What about you?

'I'm fine,' Anthony replied. 'I was glad this all worked out. Hey, did you wanna get some coffee or some food?'

'I'm chilled, I think I need to sit somewhere warm and dry off a bit.'

'Oh, OK. We could do this café I know around here. You ever been to Brava?'

Josh and Anthony crossed the street together. Anthony sized him up. Josh was tall, with grey eyes and pale, soft-looking skin, the kind of skin that reminded him of certain angels in paintings by Hans Memling. He stood in stark contrast to Anthony's more swarthy, stocky figure; a bona fide Italian-American.

Josh and Anthony crossed the street and found the café, which had a heat lamp outside. The heat from the very red lamp made steam rise from Anthony's jean jacket. Josh took a hit from his Juul and the cola-scented vapor rose like a luminous, fragrant cloud.

'Do you like mums?' Anthony said, producing from his jean jacket a small bouquet of fresh yellow flowers. 'I work at a florist's shop... so I got a couple of cuttings.'

'They're pretty, thanks,' Josh said, taking the bouquet. 'Is that a real productive job, selling flowers?'

'It can be,' Anthony replied. 'Although I'm not a florist. It was literally the only job I could get when I graduated college. I've been there now... four years I think? I'm lucky.'

Anthony watched Josh order a London Fog. He curled his cold fingers around the mug to warm them. The night had been dismal. Josh felt an ache in his back, the same one that plagued all of the other men who had stocked groceries at the QFC, a slow, insistent throbbing that could only be relieved if someone had put their hands there.

'It sounds alright, especially if you're surrounded by flowers all day.'

'Oh, everyone thinks that. I don't enjoy the flowers, though, I just cut them up. My boss does all the arranging.'

'This is the first time I've been on a date in a while,' Anthony said.

This dude needs a beard trim, Josh thought. Which was fine, because the object in Portland dating was not to find the most aesthetically pleasing boy (boys like that worked out in Beaverton, worked at Nike, drove fast cars and had the kind of Instagram accounts that used hashtags like 'curated' and 'stockists' and 'neo-minimalist'), it was to find the most vulnerable. Josh had his stipulations: he had to own a cat, had to drive a shitty car, had to give really good head. Had to be honest and had to be good looking, had to be the kind of boy who owned a jockstrap but never wore it. Anthony had been a torso on the torso wall on Grindr, just a set of pecs and some chest hair and an ab or two.

He'd seen his dick already. They'd sexted two days ago, when Anthony insisted on having phone sex with him, Anthony's voice whispering soft sexy syllables in the 2 a.m. dark as Josh stroked his dick with the blinding blue light of the phone illuminating the wine-dark sea of his apartment.

He had not expected Anthony to text him with a cursory request to meet up IRL. Josh felt like it was half-forced, this hazel-eyed softboi with his yellow mums and his London fog and his damp jean jacket.

'Actually, I'm not that naïve,' Anthony finished. 'I had a boyfriend for six years and I've dated a bunch of times just this past year. I figured it was worth a shot, just seeing if you'd wanna hang.'

'I was just thinking you were just up for a quick bang and that's it. Guys don't tend to stick.'

'I'm not sticky, am I?'

'No,' Josh replied. 'I just wasn't expecting a date.'

Anthony watched Josh finish a slice of lukewarm spinach pie. Josh said he was a vegan, although the spinach pie had butter in it. Anthony figured compromises like these were a sign of humanity; here was a vegan boy who ate butter and didn't bat an eyelash, didn't scold the barista or waitress or the server for this anti-vegan injustice.

Josh was pretty for a punk. He had beautiful skin and beautiful eyes. The patches on his jacket looked interesting. Anthony wanted to lay the jacket on his bed and peruse the patches and read their mottoes out loud, to see which bands he knew.

'I wasn't expecting to ask you out, either,' Anthony replied. 'I was thinking you'd say no.'

'I'm not that type of person,' Josh replied, not looking up as he wiped his hands on the paper napkin. 'I've learned that being an asshole to people who are looking for heart space creates a lot of bad karma.'

'Really,' Anthony replied with a chuckle. 'Any examples?'

Josh hesitated for a moment. 'Well, there was this one guy I met, and he wanted to hook up. He happened to be into kink. I'm OK with kink, but I'd never done his type of kink before, so of course it was super awkward when he just expected me to be his dom or whatever.

Anyway the date went bad, and I told a friend about it, and like, the next week, I got hit by a car crossing Burnside.'

Anthony almost spit out his tea. 'Are you serious?' Josh nodded.

'I'm so sorry,' Anthony replied. 'But, not consenting to his kink couldn't have been like, being cruel. Telling your friend about it would be OK if you were dishing about it.'

'But I wasn't,' Josh replied. 'I was like, legit disrespecting his kink. He was looking for someone to be intimate with. I guess I wasn't in good enough headspace to make that commitment, I guess.'

Anthony said nothing.

'What was your boyfriend like?' Josh said to Anthony as they walked back to Anthony's house.

'Handsome. A total burnout. He was a psychiatric nurse. He made 200K a year and I never saw him.'

'Did you guys share your place?'

'He had an apartment in the Pearl that I dreaded moving into,' Anthony replied. 'I grew up here. 92nd and Halsey. I didn't want to live in the Pearl. I didn't want to do Portland gay shit like all of his pharma bro friends were doing.'

Josh nodded. The rain had abated and the dark sidewalk was covered with leaves and puddles. Anthony had insisted on walking arm-in-arm because he thought it was cute. It felt cute. It felt like Anthony was different, like he was a real person. A boy from 92nd and Halsey, the kind of neighborhood that you could have a barbecue and eat pho in, the kind of boy who looked like he worked out but actually just drank IPAs and biked a lot.

'You seem really sweet,' Anthony said. 'I like that you throw pots. Cool hobby.'

'It's not just a hobby—it's my art.'

They trod over a big puddle, their reflections shimmering under the glare of a streetlight.

'I'm sorry,' Anthony replied. 'I didn't know... I'm sure it's beautiful art.'

Josh stopped for a second, adjusted his scarf.

'I have to be honest with you,' Josh said, pausing. 'I have two partners. Mark and Jason. I'm committed to them and we're in an open triad.'

Anthony felt a confession like this coming. He kept walking. 'I'm fine with that. Are you?'

Anthony lived in a small, spare house in Montavilla with mismatched furniture and a pile of muddy boots at the door. Anthony had hung a portrait he had painted of his grandmother over the fireplace.

Sereno

'You can take your shoes off, if you want,' Anthony said. He slipped off his boots and threw them into the pile. A calico cat sauntered out of the kitchen door and meowed.

'That's Autumn,' Anthony replied. 'She's my roommate's cat but she's real nice.'

The cat hesitated, looked up at Josh, flicked its tail, and walked back into the kitchen.

Anthony took off his jean jacket and hung it on the wall. Josh did the same and for a moment, he saw Anthony's bare midriff as the jacket came off him, the telltale, sensual trail of dark hair that ran down his chest and his stomach. Josh felt like a grey gnome compared to him, a merman whose wet grey flesh could not be kissed by the sun in the way Anthony's had.

'Do you want a glass of wine?' Anthony said from the kitchen.

'What do you have?' Josh said, sitting on Anthony's couch.

'How do you feel about a Cab? Does a Cab sound good to you?'

'Tannins,' Josh replied. 'What about a white?'

'A Riesling,' Anthony said. 'I have one uncorked bottle.' He walked out of the kitchen with the bottle in hand.

'That's fine.'

Anthony reappeared with two glasses, the Riesling and a box of apple fritters.

'You can't serve Riesling without a dessert. This is vegan, by the way.'

'Cute.'

'I was only concerned for you,' Anthony replied, sitting down on the couch.

He poured the wine in to the glasses and toasted him.

'To the clusterfuck that is Grindr,' he said.

They clinked the glasses together.

Under the warm lamplight of the bedroom Anthony looked inviting and kind. The bedroom was simple, the walls a shade of beige, almost bone. The color some enterprising interior designer might call bisque. Anthony had worn a waffle henley with a smooth hand. Josh could feel Anthony's chest hair crinkle under the fabric when he ran his hands over it. He felt his stubble brush against his pale, cool cheek. He did not merely kiss the way some timid gay boys do, as if they are kissing their grandmother as she dies, his kisses were earthy like he was. Anthony kissed Josh the way Josh wanted to be kissed: slowly, affectively, with intent.

But things changed when Anthony slipped off his shirt and began unbuckling his jeans, and started unbuckling Josh's jeans, too.

'I can't do this,' Josh said, pushing Anthony's hands away. 'Anthony, you're sweet, but I don't fuck on the first date.'

'Oh, OK. Well then, we can just cuddle if you want.'

'I'm OK with cuddling and kissing…' Josh hesitated for a bit. 'Where did you learn how to kiss so good?'

'So well, you mean,' Anthony replied. 'I've had practice.'

'What do you mean, "practice"?'

Anthony laughed. 'Well what do you want me to tell you? I mean, like, pillows and shit. Dudes that I've dated. Ex-boyfriends I've had.'

'It's very nice,' Josh said, smiling gently. 'My partners never like to kiss me.'

'Why is that?'

Josh sighed. 'I mean, once, when we all met, and the romance was very strong it was kissing all the time. But as time has gone on, it's become more about being intimate with each other in other ways. There's also an emotional component to kissing I feel you can't share with a stranger. And bears can be sloppy kissers, sometimes.'

'So Mark and Jason are bears, then.'

Josh nodded quietly. 'Is that a problem?'

'Not for me,' Anthony replied.

'Anyway,' Josh replied. 'You're a great kisser.'

'I would like to kiss you much more. I mean, I can't promise I won't be sloppy...'

'But you aren't sloppy at all,' Josh replied.

'Your ceiling is trippy,' Josh said, looking up at the plaster ceiling above Anthony's large bed. 'Do you ever get stoned and just stare at it?'

It was almost 2 a.m. and they'd been talking for three hours.

'I've never done that, and I get stoned a lot.' He didn't say anything for a long time. 'Did you bring any weed with you?'

'Yeah, I usually carry some around for pain management.'

'Ah,' Anthony replied. 'You must work hard a lot. I can give you a massage one of these days, if you want.'

Josh squeezed Anthony's hand.

'That'd be real nice, you're real sweet.'

They shared a joint and stared up at the ceiling together.

'You know,' Anthony said, 'I don't miss my ex at all. I thought I was in love with him for the longest time. But now I think I just enjoyed being able to sleep with another body in bed.'

'Kinda like now?'

'Yeah, like now. I used to like reading poetry in bed, right before turning in. I used to write a lot of poetry when he and I first met. Then I stopped, I can't tell you why I did.'

'Six years of writer's block seems like hell on earth.'

He didn't reply, but kept looking up at the ceiling. Finally, after a long while, he said: 'Even just one night of writer's block is enough. For the first few days after we started talking on Grindr I felt like writing poetry.'

'You're lying,' Josh replied, with a chuckle. 'You're fucking shitting me.'

'No! No I am not, actually,' Anthony replied.

'You can't be that smitten with me, it's impossible.'

'But I am,' Anthony said. 'It is possible. I wouldn't have invited you over to my house if I didn't feel the way I do.'

The lamplight was warm enough to lull Josh into closing his eyes, and before he knew it they were both asleep, snoring loudly. Josh woke up and found Anthony asleep on his side. He sat up in bed. He stood up to put on his shirt and maybe sneak out. Anthony had pulled the huge trade show blanket at the foot of his bed over his body. His hair was disheveled. The last thing Josh could remember was some weird anecdote that Anthony had related about one of François Truffault's films, maybe *À bout du souffle*, because he had mentioned riding around Paris in a drop-top car.

Breathless

He stared at Anthony in bed for a long time, watching him inhale and exhale. After about five minutes, Josh unbuckled his pants, rolled them to the floor, and got back in bed. He moved in close to wrap his arms around Anthony.

'Hi there, good morning,' Anthony whispered, half-awake.

Josh said nothing and covered himself with Anthony's blanket. He closed his eyes and tried to lull himself back to sleep. Holding someone other than Mark or Jason's body felt weird and foreign. Josh fell asleep reminding himself, in a mantra, that it wasn't "technically" cheating if you could cuddle in someone's bed in your underwear, dreaming of scenes from French new wave cinema, with someone who needed to be held. If there had ever been a moral imperative for cuddling, it was now.

The morning came on thick and grey. The rain pattered on the rooftop. When Anthony awoke at 7:30, Josh was on his back, his mouth open and a few feathers on his bare pale chest. Anthony kissed his chest very gently, until Josh awoke, rubbed his eyes, and then turned over. Anthony lay his hand on Josh's chest and fell back to sleep in the crook of his smelly armpit.

'I shouldn't have stayed,' Josh said, putting on his boots. 'Fuck, I'm gonna be late for work now.'

'It's my day off. I can take you to work.'

'But my bike?'

'I can pick you up from work too.'

'You'd do that for me?'

'Absolutely. And maybe if you want, I can make us some dinner.'

Josh smiled and put on his scarf. He stood up. 'That's real sweet, but I'm gonna have to pass. Mark and Jason and me are all having dinner tonight.'

'Oh,' Anthony replied. 'Well, I can still pick you up from work.'

'Only if you want to do that,' Josh replied. 'I mean, it's not a big deal if you can't. I can stop by and pick up my bike tonight.'

'OK,' Anthony replied. 'But let me take you to work. And I can pick you up.'

Anthony bought Josh some coffee at a Starbucks on the corner of where the QFC was. Josh slowly sipped his coffee in the car, while the windshield wipers threw off torrents of cold rain. The windows were beginning to fog. Josh was scrolling past something he was reading on Twitter, and didn't look up at Anthony.

'It was so nice having you over last night.'

'Yeah, it was for me, too.' Josh replied.

'I like falling asleep with you.'

'Nothing like French art house films as a sleepy time subject, I guess.'

Josh sniffed the mums that Anthony had given him, stowed them in the inner pocket of his jacket.

'Pretty fall flowers, funeral flowers,' Anthony said. 'It's bad luck to give someone mums, but I like the color. It's a happy color.'

'Feels like I never really get to see flowers all that much anymore. I used to date this one rich guy who always sent me flowers. Tiger lilies. He wanted a sugar baby.' Josh raised a finger as if he were clarifying something unsaid. 'A pool boy. In reality, he wanted a pool boy.'

Anthony laughed.

Josh looked at Anthony for a few seconds, and then planted a fat wet kiss on his lips.

'Meet me at four-thirty,' he said. 'I'll be waiting for you outside.'

When Josh had disappeared inside the store, Anthony sent him a Bitmoji, one that showed Anthony offering a bouquet of rainbow colored hearts. Anthony pulled out of the parking lot and headed home, his heart feeling full, satisfied, optimistic. The rain was falling in heavy sheets now, descending like a cold grey cloud, flooding the world except for the warm space where Anthony was. He felt invincible.

Anthony proceeded to the red light, the last one before he turned off into the street where his house was. He watched the blinking red signal, looking for other drivers in the four-way intersection, and when he saw none, proceeded through the intersection.

A white Ford F150 pickup truck hydroplaned through the intersection, slamming directly into the driver's side of Anthony's car. A blur of broken glass and rain and blood and metal. The last thing that Anthony saw before he got hit—the last thing that Anthony felt—was his cell phone buzz in his pocket. Josh had seen the Bitmoji, and had responded.

When the paramedics arrived, Anthony was unconscious and the other driver was dead.

Josh had had a normal day. He ate some red pepper soup for lunch at the vegan deli next door, had thought of the next thing he would say when he saw Anthony again. He finished up his shift and sat on the bench outside the QFC. The rain had abated and was now falling in a light drizzle. He was looking forward to seeing Anthony, to looking into his eyes, to feeling his chest hair, the warm fuzzy feeling of the trade show blanket with the tiger on it. Four o'clock came and Josh looked for Anthony's green Subaru in the parking lot, expecting him to show up early. He got up and walked around the parking lot to see if he could find him. Four-thirty arrived and the traffic had picked up. Josh got up and walked to the end of the parking lot, watched the bus come and go.

Josh went back to the bench in front of the QFC and sat down again. It was now five-fifteen.

Anthony didn't seem like one of those guys who ghost you after the first date, he told himself. Anthony would inevitably show up. He had to.

Sereno

The Fifth Season

ECEMBER 26, 2008. IT DOESN'T FEEL like Christmas, because Christmas is without its cold-season requisites: ice and snow. We could have watched the tide roll in on the Island from the safety of the porch at the beach house you and I share, but you are gone. I shield my eyes and look into the sky filled with torn white clouds. White laundry flutters in the wind. My mother says, "I've got one more sheet for you," and together we pin the sheet to the line; for a brief moment I am caught up in a wall of wet cotton impregnated with the smell of detergent, someone else's springtime fantasy. The sun is low and the south wind is blowing. The wind in the trees is what you hear. Two in the afternoon, and the air is warm, soft, dry, a paradisiacal zephyr from the outer waters of the Gulf.

We are taking down the Christmas decorations. It will all go into one Sterilite container. The act of removing the decorations is deflating, depressing. My mother does not want to do it, but it must be done. She has her routines, her need for order and cleanliness, and we must comply if we are to have peace. The concrete on the front porch is still wet with morning dew. While taking down the strands of white icicle lights, I remember those late spring days when you used to visit my house late at night, when you had nothing to do. You would not walk into the house, but wait patiently until I had unlatched the front door and walked out into the dark to meet you. In your car we'd kiss for something like ten minutes, and I could smell the garlic that you'd eaten for dinner on your breath and in your skin; I could smell the Azzaro on the nape of your neck, the sweat in the cleft of your pecs, but most of all I could smell the Hong Kong orchid petals crushed under the soles of your Nikes. While I am taking down the wreath from the front door I imagine you standing behind the screen door, asking to come in. You always asked politely to come in because you somehow knew the fractured dynamics of family and culture here. I put the wreath in the plastic box. Mom says, "Make sure to stack it so I can pull it out next year."

We have Christmas ham sandwiches and tamales for dinner. Mom watches an old Rankin/Bass special on TV and irons my little brother's work slacks. He will have to return to work tomorrow at The Home Depot. I will tarry here, until the middle of January, when I can finally return to school. You call me from Dallas and inform me that the Christmas party you attended was a magnificent failure, precipitated by a political argument gone haywire and too much badly prepared food. There was turkey and stuffing, you say, but someone forgot to remove the giblets. What you do not tell me is that you are calling me from a room at the Omni, because you do not want anyone to know that you didn't go because you were depressed. Depressed because I could not join you, depressed because I could not hold your hand and smile at you from across a long table. You do not tell me that your Christmas dinner is room service. You do not tell me that you plan to hook up with your ex later that evening, who promptly ghosts you at 2 AM to go to a drag ball afterparty.

The sun sets. It is cool and wet and blue in the garden again. The planet Saturn rises in the eastern December sky and shines like a bright silver nail affixed to the darkening sphere of the sky. A few errant wisps of pink cirrus alight in the west over the deep blue of twilight. The rest of the neighborhood has Christmas lights still up. In my house, however, the Christmas tree is packed away in multiple boxes with all of its attendant splendor. The party is over. The year is just a quickly fading memory, and the days to come are mostly dark, mostly twilit, days made of midnight blue and silver, full of reviewal but mostly full of regret. I will watch a rerun of *Jesús, El Niño Dios*. It will rain on the last two days of the year. I will be outside watching the sky get slowly greyer and darker, I will hear thunder in the afternoon, and I will watch as the first fat drops of rain splash on the concrete of the front porch. I will watch a news report about the Huichol pilgrimage to Wirikuta. I will think about you while I watch the sun emerge from a cloud. I will think about holding your hand, about getting into a car I don't own and driving to the beach house I don't live in. I will think about finding you in the hammock on the porch, asleep in your swim trunks or your underwear, I will think about the still summer evenings on the beach where we saw all of the stars.

You call me the next evening. You ask me if I had a good Christmas. I respond that yes, I have, that Uncle Scott has given me some new clothing and a new bracelet for me to wear, and that all in all, we had a satisfying Christmas dinner. I sit on the stiff plywood bench under the carport outside and we talk about the night sky, about the compilation of Debussy your parents gave you, about dead relatives and dead pets, about certain trees and certain landscapes we know. I tell you about almanacs and constellations I can see from the backyard, about how I really just want a pair of binoculars to look at the stars with. The night is getting gradually cooler and more serene, and I can feel the dew begin to settle on the ground again. I know the fog will return from the coast. You tell me that you will drive down from Austin to be with me, so that we can spend the New Year together.

The Fifth Season

I smile and close my eyes and inhale deeply, gratified with the singular privilege of getting to see you during the holidays. You tell me you love me. I am lulled into a sense of safety, of incipient repose, and retire to my room that evening hopelessly, desperately in love with you and the world again, convinced that it is a kinder and more beautiful place, in spite of the distance between us.

After you hang up the phone you sit on the red leather couch in your parents' house in Dallas, not knowing what to think or feel. Everyone is getting ready to go out to the ice-skating rink. Your nephew tugs on your sweater sleeve and asks you to come with him. You shrug it off the first couple of times, but then you resolve to go for his sake. At the ice-skating rink, you think of how nice it would be if our worlds were a little less different, if I did not live in South Texas, and if you did not live in Dallas. You fall on the ice a couple of times, everyone falls, everyone laughs, gets up, continues to perambulate in an ellipse in the rink around a gigantic sparkling poinsettia wreath hanging from the ceiling of the mall. In the parking lot you grip the steering wheel of the car, breathe deeply and try to ward off the impending sense of angst that is washing over you. You will have to drive back home alone, and there is no one to talk to. Your ex does not want to talk to you. Your other ex is in Florida at a circuit party and is too stoned or drunk to talk to you. And I am asleep.

Instead, you stay up until midnight. You watch an experimental film. You go to Whataburger and buy a cheeseburger and some fries and a big Coke, and then after the Coke you sit there in the dark, in your car, wondering what to do. You go home to your kitchen to pour yourself some wine and sit down in the living room, and, without taking your eyes off the Christmas tree, you drink the wine, you suffocate a sob. Another year has come to an end, and there we are, alone in the dark. Years later, after we separate for the final time, you meet me on a terrace in Portland and you ask me what was so appealing about those final days. I tell you that it was the first and only time I've ever really known what true love looked and felt like, even if it was love from afar. That evening is gentle, not unlike those spring nights where we could smell the flowers opening in the night air. You put your arms around me and sigh, and for a moment I am back with you on the beach, with the sound of the surf in my ears and the taste of salt in my mouth, and inside me the tide swells, breaks on the shore of my memories, recedes; the memory of those winter days that felt like spring remains, a solitary glowing ember in the ashes of the extinguished past.

The Fifth Season

A Kind of Blue

 CAN'T WAIT TO SEE YOU AGAIN. HE TEXTS this TO me as I arise, my bleary eyes closing against the distant blue of dawn, and there, all alone, I tell him that I miss him. The blue is a pastel blue. A sad blue. A blue that is more of a paradox than an actual color, a color of oblivion. It is a kind of blue that you might find at 11 PM on a Miles Davis track, at 6 PM in someone's pool in a rich house in LA, in a pool of jacaranda petals. In this blue, I tell him (and no one in particular) that I miss him. *I can't wait to see you again.*

The guy with the brown hair and the clear skin and the silver crucifix in his hairy chest croons to me a particular line from a Cole Porter song: *go do that voodoo that you do so well* and as he is driving me home, he is telling me how much he loved the last boyfriend who was clueless enough to cheat on him, and how much loves me. In all my relationships, the stories are all the same. Never a victim, but they all played the role like an artist. There was, for example, the one summer in Italy in his junior year of college that he always told me about, the one he spent studying frescoes of martyrs in Santo Stefano Rotondo, or caressing his then-girlfriend's hair in Campitelli while studying a mosaic in what used to be Santa Maria Antiqua, while thousands of miles away I languished in the heat of my backyard in South Texas, playing with the dog in the light that was silver, that was lavender, that light that always somehow faded to a deep and distant blue in the cool waters of the Gulf, me in love with another man, me unaware of the philosophical airs of this current boyfriend who tells me, in the dark of my room, that he will never find happiness, even if it's with me.

Pour me another cocktail, someone says, in the dream that I have, in which I am sure I am eating figs and what looks like a tray of antipasti, on a table with an immaculately starched white linen tablecloth, on which sits a vase of blue carnations—that is, white carnations dyed blue. When I wake up it is 3 AM on 15 August, the feast of the Assumption of Mary, and I feel that the carnations and the white tablecloth and maybe even the olives are mundane reminders of the miracle of Mary's leave-taking, her heavenly journey into the bluest of summer skies, big puffy white clouds passing up and before her. He likes to remind me that during Ferragosto, this time during August, everyone leaves on vacation.

In bed that night he tells me to hold him tight and a few tears roll down my face and fall on his back and he kisses my salty tears away as I hold him there, never wanting to let go of him. *Why are you crying* he says and I respond *I don't know why maybe it's because I'm happy. You're so full of shit* he says, chuckling, but he is right, all of this maybe is just me overreacting.

Freshly shaved and showered after the oppressive and still afternoon in the office, I wait for him in the lush green of my backyard, watching the blues cascade down over white and grey clouds that roll over the valley like silent angels watching for the approach of the gates of the night. I am living through my own version of Baudelaire's poem about the evening, about the fountains that adorn the silken prisons of the marble-clad past. In my mind I am remembering the art song composed by Debussy, with my own ecstatic refrain: I am the gilt angel that stands on the threshold of time. I am the fountain, I am the rose.

Last night he and I tried to play bridge. We tried to play because our much smarter friends like to pretend that bridge is a respectable game, a game that well-off couples play, in order to offset their competitive edge by inviting a demonstrably lesser set of opponents to fraternize with them. Our friends made silly compliments and served us fruit and cheese, and in the windows of their house we saw the same blue, filtered through a haze of tall bushes. I saw the evening star rise above them. The twilight. Our failure, rendered in filigree, every little shadow played out in the hand.

I always imagined that I'd live in a house painted blue, that looked out on beach like the house I used to live in ten years ago. That house was white and looked clean from the outside, and had a kitchen that everyone was forbidden to use—partly because my ex-boyfriend's mother insisted that greasy food stains don't really ever wash out of white wood.

See, in the house I want it is always twilight. The blue is everywhere, even in the wood, even in the banisters of the stairs and even in the basins in the upstairs bathroom. There are white roses that are blue in this twilight in the little garden that faces the street and a chenille bedspread and the bedroom there is also blue, also needlessly blue with little copper touches, little ringlets of coppery fire, nightlights that are blue, noises that are so helplessly blue.

After a few minutes under the lights at the supermarket we pick out a pot roast and some red bell peppers and a parsnip and walk back to his place, as the blue light from the twilight shimmers over the hills in the west, resplendent and menacing and brilliant in their cobalt curtains, like the windows at Chartres.

Because this is Portland and it is March, this a rare blue evening, the kind that you tell secrets to your friends to on. He is wearing white clogs that he swears are good for your posture.

A Kind of Blue

We pass through the beaded curtain made of white nacre disks to the kitchen, where the blue light is so low that it inches in over the white six-by-six windows, into the stainless steel sink. He makes dinner and I put on some João Donato and he kisses my cheek and when he does this I can feel the sting of his stubble.

On the way back home that we turn a corner and took a different route. He lets me put my hand into the pocket of his blue denim jacket. This is also blue, faded like a piece of sea glass.

I will see him again tonight, when the world is blue, when the twilight fades and the world grows dim and fuzzy, yet oddly retains its warmth and familiarity. In this summer blue, I will find him again, smiling as he sips from a cocktail, reminding me to finish the first volume of Proust over a pulled pork supper. In my mouth, there is the sting of white wine, also tinged blue in its glass from the paper lanterns above, the blue shade of twilight on the white linen tablecloth with blue splotches, the blue of the world that never seems too literal, the hasty yet relaxed crawl towards the end of night.

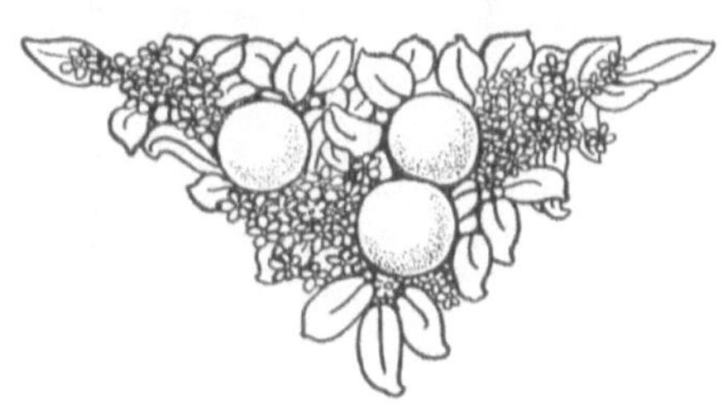

Sereno

Sister Annie, Going West

HE HEAT REVERBERATES IN SISTER Annie's mind; it shimmers like electric air above the grey-green sea. First the train passes through the city with its tenements, its air that stinks of refuse and sewage, passing row after row of brick house with slate roofs and chimney stacks that blur one by one until they are all brown sticks against the pale smoggy blue sky of late July, 1878.

Philadelphia disappears from Sister Annie's view finally after an hour, and the world is leafy and green again; she remembers the fields of chamomile and bachelor's button of her childhood. She compares those fields in her memory to the gentle rolling fields of western Pennsylvania, where farmers leer at the train as it passes through the grades into worn hills strewn with rocks and trees. She looks back at Mother Superior reading from her prayerbook, nodding off into sleep as the Pullman car sways gently on the rails. Two white men look down on her and puff away at their cigars. The porter, chocolate-dark and compliant, offers her lemonade. 'Where you comin' from?' the porter asks. 'Who you know out in California?'

'I'm a nun,' Sister Annie says, gently, as if she is telling a secret. To prove her point, she pulls out a rosary and fingers the crucifix with a thumb and forefinger. The porter looks at her, shakes his head and walks away.

The only thing Sister Annie has known all her life is Philadelphia. She remembers the smell of offal cooking in grease, the sound of the blacksmith cursing God and man in the streets, the acrid stench of death in the slaughterhouse, the steaming rivers of blood flowing from dead horses kicking their lives out on the cobblestones. She struggles to remember her dead mother's face, the face of her dead sister (murdered, dumped in Baltimore Harbor) and the calloused hands of her dead brother (murdered, at Antietam). She does not know who her father was, but the stories her mother told her relate that he is kind-eyed, virile, strong, a man of tropical sensibilities and urban sophistication. Born free, you must understand. Never a slave.

The porter pushes a cart full of tea sandwiches through the aisle. A very nice man, a fellow Catholic, with an unusual gentility, pays for Sister Annie's meal.

Sister Annie, Going West

'Are you going out West to teach Negroes and Indians to read?' he asks. She has heard questions like these before, they are all the same. Sister Annie nods, gently, but does not look up at him.

There are many stops before the train finally accelerates out of Pennsylvania: Brooksville, Eagle, Paoli where Sister Annie and Mother Superior dine on potted roast chicken and new potatoes and a slice of chocolate cake that the sisters have baked for her. The train stops in a nameless twilight town with a white steepled church and a bunch of butternut trees. The porter delivers the newspaper, and Mother Superior squints through her pince-nez glasses to read about that den of sinners known as the US Congress. The children crowd around the windows, black and white, sticks and balls in hand, to ask why Sister Annie wears a funny hat. Sister Annie closes the shade and tries to sleep. An hour later the train is moving and everything is loud and dim. A cool breeze blows through the half-opened car window. She can smell the rain.

The next day the train is in Ohio and Indiana and the rain streaks the window. Everything is grey and wet, and for a moment it feels like a humid October afternoon. She remembers the convent in Philadelphia, the smell of starched linen and the polish of wooden veneers, the cool dark of the chapel where she prays to God. The train passes through Cincinnati, resinous and fragrant with the scent of maples, and she sees Black men and women in buckboards with fancy hats on the way to Bible study in the rain. The children run alongside the train track and yell incoherent nonsense to the nonplussed businessmen, the ladies who look away in disgust and sniff their tussymussies in polite contempt. Mother Superior's fingers course her rosary beads, and the two of them recite the Regina Coeli together as they pass through a city full of Italians peddling tomatoes and grapes and Greeks selling lemons and oregano, and dour-faced white women with market baskets shuffling on walkways made of planks past beautiful dark-skinned boys shoveling coal into pails. At Vincennes, Indiana, Mother Superior spies two priests step on with just suitcases that the porter struggles to pack away.

'A good sign,' she says. 'And also a bad sign.'

'Why?' Sister Annie says.

'We're almost to the West, but also amongst Mormons.'

The land abruptly flattens in Indiana and rolls out gently like a blanket spread out against heaven, Indian land. Not to the Mississippi yet, but almost there. The train groans on the rail in the heat. Sister Annie pats her brow with an embroidered handkerchief. Mother Superior splashes cool water on her face. The conductor announces that they will be stopping for refreshment at a river.

'A godsend,' Mother Superior says, relieved.

In the plains the heat is ferocious and unforgiving. Somewhat like the people, when provoked to unjust anger. Sister Annie thinks of the men who lynched her school friend and her husband out here, for trying to buy a nag. You don't do that out there in those parts, a white man told Sister Annie once. She can't remember where she met him—whether it was just right after the War, when she was young, or whether it was a dying man in the hospital, or maybe a man passing through. *You don't pretend you're on equal footing with white people. I've never been prejudiced. Not one prejudiced bone in my body. If you ask me that was wrong, what they done to your friend. But you don't presume to place yourself on the square and narrow with white folks. They just won't have it.*

Here is where Sister Annie recognizes nothing. There is sky and grass, and rails. And cows. She sees an Indian dying in the street on the way down to the water hole. Mother Superior takes his temperature and gives him a bit of food, pays the doctor in the town to give him a bed to die in.

'I don't take Indians in, there's no telling what he'll do if he gets better.'

'You don't need to worry,' Mother Superior says, pressing the money into the doctor's hand.

'I'm a Lutheran, just so you know. I don't take money from no Papists.'

'It shouldn't matter who I am,' she replies. 'Just take the money.'

'Who do you think you are?' the doctor asks.

'It's not important,' Mother says. 'A good Samaritan.'

One of the priests from Vincennes, Father Dyer, rolls a cigarette out in front of the hotel where the Indian is dying. The other priest, Father Gerard, is giving the dying Indian viaticum.

'Where are you headed?'

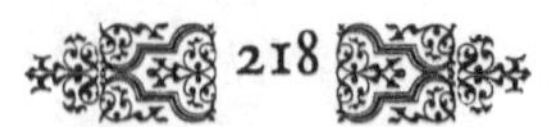

Sister Annie, Going West

'California. And then Washington territory.'

'Long way,' Father Dyer says, lighting the cigarette.

'You?'

'New Mexico territory,' he says. 'I'm not ready for the heat. Rather prodigious, much more so than what they lead on.'

'It's rather nice, depending on where you go in New Mexico.'

'You've been?'

'Oh yes,' Mother Superior replies sweetly. 'I taught my first classes there in Taos, after the Mexican War. I've come back east to fetch Sister Annie here to send her out to a new convent. In a town called Roseland.'

'Never have heard of it,' Father Dyer says. 'The originals of the place will be in for a surprise,' he chuckles.

The other priest comes out and shakes his head.

'We should call the undertaker.'

'How long ago did he pass?'

Sereno

Father Gerard checks his pocket watch. 'Some ten minutes ago.'

The heat breaks that evening. A cool wind comes with a night fog that dissipates before the front of a violent thunderstorm. Rain hammers out a tattoo on the leaky tin roof. In the hotel room, Sister Annie cannot stay asleep, so she watches as the lightning streaks and flashes across the sky from behind a window, and feels the thunder rumble down to her bones.

The undertaker rolls out a coffin the next morning. A few women huddle across the street to see what will happen. The priests follow the wagon, in surplice, stole and biretta, reading the breviary. Mother Superior and Sister Annie go as far out as the burying ground, which abuts a tepid, foul-smelling stream. They bury the Indian at three in the afternoon and pay the undertaker for a tombstone.

'Did you know his name?' they ask the undertaker.

'Indian Joe,' the undertaker replies.

Sister Annie looks at the grey sky overhead, and closes her eyes in prayer.

Sister Annie, Going West

St Louis is a Sodom, roiling under the sun. Sister Annie sees wealthy-looking Black men in tweed suits spill from overcrowded rail cars to head over to the saloons for the three o'clock drink. The Mississippi is a stagnant, fetid mass of still, dirty water over which clouds of insects nervously hover. She smells the scent of chili and green bell pepper and frying tripe wafting from the shoddy shacks lining a muddy street. The smokestacks of factories and foundries belch fat columns of black smoke as far as the eye can see. The smell is sickening.

'Don't close the window,' Mother Superior says. 'We'll die of the heat if we do.'

A new conductor comes aboard and spends a long time looking at Sister Annie's ticket.

'Who told you that could sit up here, girl?'

'I did,' Mother Superior replies, firmly. 'We don't travel alone.'

'I didn't ask you,' the conductor says. 'You can't be up here. You need to get up and get on back. That's where we keep the colored folk.'

'She isn't going anywhere,' Mother Superior says.

'The conductor is losing his patience and clears his voice.

'I don't think you *heard* me, ma'am. This Negro woman is forbidden on the train. Now I don't care if you're the Queen of Roumania and she's Princess Caraboo. If you don't like it, both of you should get off the train. Don't make me get the sergeant-at-arms, you hear?'

The porter looks helpless as he takes their bags and sets them down gently on the platform.

'Beg your pardon, ma'am,' the porter says over and over again. 'Beg your pardon. Beg your pardon.'

'I will have to write the Archbishop.'

'I'm sorry, Mother—'

'There's nothing to be sorry about, my daughter. You did nothing wrong. Perhaps I did wrong. Maybe the Lord wanted us to ride with the other people in the back.'

'You were only doing what you thought was right,' Sister Annie. 'Besides. I would have gotten up and gone if he wanted me to.'

Sister Annie, Going West

'But you didn't want to,' Mother Superior says. 'And there's nothing wrong with not wanting to go to a place you don't want to go.'

They walk to a hotel, alone, in the early evening, and pass rows of tenements and Chinese laundries. Mother Superior does not sleep that night on the uncomfortable cast-iron bed, but pens a letter to the Archbishop. She hands the note to an errand boy who runs across town to the Archbishop. At seven in the morning, Sister Annie is spreading jam on her toast when the boy comes back, with another note.

Mother Superior reads it and sits back in her chair.

'His Excellency has made protest to the railroad officials via telegraph.' She folds the note and puts it in her bag. 'They have reimbursed our tickets. We leave tomorrow evening.'

In the afternoon, the nuns walk to the Cathedral alone. The men do not leer and gawk at them like they did in Vincennes. Downtown St Louis seems like a nice place to be a nun. Everyone keeps to themselves, even the Irish boys washing their horses and scrubbing the carriages, even the Black and Spanish boys corralling the horses in the carriage-house, even the German and Italian girls skipping down the block, singing to themselves and carrying armfuls of fabric and bread. The breeze picks up as they get closer to the river and for a moment Sister Annie smells linden and roses, someone's potted chicken spilling over a fire, and she hears the sounds of mothers calling in their children to eat dinner. The Cathedral in St Louis is cool and dark and still, a cold grey temple with cool pink walls inside and no one praying. Sister Annie thinks of her sister laughing in the splash of cold water from a creek they played in as a child, her mother mending a dress, the bright world of a June day mottled with green grass and little pink roses. The sunset brings a cool breeze into town and they walk back after Mass saying nothing, just as the lamps are being lit and the dust is rising in an angry, defiant little cloud that whirls itself into oblivion on the street.

The station agent stands in the doorway of their cabin on the train headed to California. The air is thick with the smell of axel grease and manure.

'She's not going to be a problem,' Mother Superior says.

'I didn't think she was,' the station agent says.

'Please sir, we are two nuns. We don't aim to bother anyone. I'm sure you've dealt with our ilk before. We are most happy to keep to ourselves, provided there isn't anyone to make trouble for us,' Mother Superior replies.

'Now you listen here! You best not be giving nobody any trouble, you hear me, girl?' the station agent says to Sister Annie. He has stopped looking at Mother Superior, who is shocked into silence. 'No carrying on. No loud talking. You bother one of the other patrons, I'll toss your black ass into the street where no one will render aid to you.'

The station agent slams the door to the cabin shut.

Mother Superior's frown eases. She chuckles.

'We should pray for him,' she says. 'He looks like he needs it.'

The train pulls away and Sister Annie heaves a sigh of relief. She looks out of the window. The sky is pink and purple. She watches it sink into a deep-blue against the black edge of the horizon with its smell of new-mown hay and its flickering green clouds of lightning bugs.

Four days in and they have left Missouri and Kansas, blighted with heat and struck dumb with the sound of cicadas buzzing in the locust trees, its grey rocks and its yellow ground. Kansas is nothing like she has ever seen, a flat wasteland with very little green, except for a few stark places where the trees shoot up like hands cupped to heaven as if to beg God for rain. Sister Annie drifts off to hand somewhere in-between chapters of *Introduction to the Devout Life*, she is transported in her dreams back east to the foggy dark of a Baltimore on the cusp of war, young men torching the houses of black and brown people, driving them into the street.

Sister Annie sees her sister pushed through a crowd of angry boys, stripped, slapped, beaten to a pulp, pushed into Baltimore Harbor, her legs kicking in the green-black sea, her body floating amidst the whoops and hollers of the crowd, the black starless sky, the belts of waves buffeting her swollen body, the flies that hover over her lips. The nightmare is enough to jolt her just as she sees the distant mountains appear over the horizon, Mother Superior reciting the Hours quietly in her monotone.

'A nightmare,' she tells Mother Superior.

'Pray with me,' Mother Superior replies.

They pray together. The landscape blurs together in a haze of pink and purple twilight, the peaks of the distant mountains growing closer and closer by the hour, until they loom over her in Denver, in a bosom of pines that whisper in the dry south wind. The train comes to a stop somewhere in the Rockies, and she can feel a sort of lightness, a sense of repose, wash over her. She rests her eyes and in the dim light of the Pullman car she hears Mother Superior recite a litany to Our Lady of Loretto, gently, and the words wash over her like waves, *have mercy on us, have mercy on us, have mercy on us.* Carefully, she draws the quilt over her tiny body, her dark fingers slipping over the rosary beads. Mother Superior stays up that night, and caresses her face like a mother in the dark. She says, *God bless you, daughter, first of my own flock to come to the West.*

And there, amid the mute granite masses of broken time, Sister Annie realizes that this west is all hers now, her very own country, where the pain and the misery of the East can finally dissipate in the golden light of the west, where there is endless freedom in the cool fresh air, where nothing inhibits the waters passing through the lost and undiscovered country where the light's fingers reach into the pines to touch the place where angels inscribed the burnished name of Almighty God.

Solitudes

N HAPPIER TIMES I USED TO WRITE HOME. I'd take down a notebook to one of the tables under the big concrete pergola facing the sea and write my mother a letter home. I don't remember what I would write to her about. Back then I had a job that'd let me take hour lunches, and after I'd sent the letter I'd walk down the sandy concrete promenade and watch the sun glint off the whitecaps. The benefit of living on the coast, you see, is that the sea offers its own palette of watercolors. And what you don't get from the sea, the mainland and the lagoon makes up for in spades: the pinks of bougainvilleas, the hot orange of royal poincianas, the sticky humid greens of palms, the mauves and taupes of storm clouds hovering off the coast in the evening after the sea breeze moves ashore on hot, sticky, sometimes windless days.

It didn't matter if there were people on the promenade or not—I felt immensely, luxuriously alone. My boss let me wear the same two white guayabera shirts almost every day and during lunch I'd unbutton the third button to let the sea breeze caress with me in the way that it can only caress a man. I don't remember what I ate then (if I had tacos I had the same tacos that I have now from the same food cart at the opposite end of the promenade), but one thing I do remember is the weather. When the wind blew it took sand and sea salt and deposited it in gentle drifts of fine brown sediment at the base of the church, in the pockets of the brick pavers of the promenade, sometimes in the folds of palm fronds. It was always in your shoes, even if you were inside all day. Every afternoon, like clockwork, an inky wave would move in from the eastern part of the bay and darken the green brow of the shore, drop its silky grey curtains of rain, and maybe a waterspout or two.

During the summer the heat was unreal. Ninety, ninety-one degrees at nine o'clock in the morning on the mainland. The sun, of course, glistened over the liquid quicksilver of the morning sea. And almost every morning during the summer I'd see him walk from one end of the promenade to the other, taking his surfboard and a towel with him, to the beach to take a morning swim. I would watch him during my lunch breaks. My eyes trained themselves on his broad tanned back as it dived in between crests, the way water spilled rivulets down his brown sugar shoulders, his wet hair.

One day I finished lunch early and I sat under the pergola watching him surf. He sat at the far end of a picnic table and shook the sand from his feet.

Solitudes

'Nice day, isn't it?' he said to me.

I was taken back by his forwardness and almost ignored him.

'Oh yes,' I said. 'It's very nice.'

'Really good surf out there, too.'

'Are you out every day?'

He had green eyes. His skin was darker than I thought.

'I've got to stay on top of my game,' he replied, before getting up. 'You have a nice day, now,' he said.

I saw that boy surf in all weather. If it rained, he went when the rain let up and the skies were laminate. If it was hot, he went before the sun could traverse the promenade—if there were no shadows under the palm trees, it was too hot to go out in bare feet on the sand. But in the fine, sweet afternoons—when the sun had descended so that it sat over the lagoon in warm, careless splendor—I'd get a full view of his chest and stomach in the midst of those green waves. I wanted him the way you want a drink after the end of a long day. I'd return to my office and do whatever it was I did for work, but at the end of the day, I'd take my shoes off and wait for him to come to the pergola to readjust his junk in his swim shorts and say hello to me.

'You again,' he said to me once. 'Too hot out for you?'

'No,' I replied. 'I come here to people watch.'

'People watch,' he replied, bemused. 'Does that mean girls? Do you come here to look at girls?'

'No,' I said, and walked away.

Eventually, I figured, he was on to me. I didn't know how old he was, and I didn't want to. If he was a teenager I knew how to keep my distance. If he were older, I could also keep my distance. I would look at my brown skin and my black hair in the mirror in my apartment, run a brush through to get the flyaway parts to stay down (impossible in a humid climate). He'd never want me, I said. I went to the gym, did my pushups in the morning, and when I wanted to visit the nude beach to tan with the fat old tourist penguins, I did so with the understanding that no one would want me there, because no one was longing for me the way I was longing for the nameless young man who stood under the pergola in the late afternoons, rearranging his junk in the sopping swim trunks he wore.

And yet, he'd look at me in his visits to the pergola, look at me for the longest time, smile mysteriously and sip from his long green bottle of Sprite. Day after day I'd process expense reports in a low ceilinged office with a telex machine and a bad internet connection to the mainland, waiting for the moment when the office clock would inch towards one, when I could emerge onto the bright promenade with its coral-colored granite seawall, its brutalist pergola facing the sea, the green-grey sea speaking to my enervated lust in a dull roar that said his name.

One day, he waited for me.

'Why are you here all alone?'

'Why does it matter?' I replied.

'OK, fine,' he said. 'I'll leave you alone.'

He turned away and started walking toward the shore.

I said, 'I used to like surfing, too. I just don't do it anymore. How old are you?'

'Twenty-three,' he replied.

He had confessed to seeing me emerge every day from the office and undoing the buttons on my guayabera

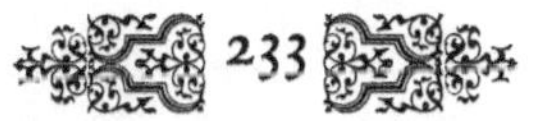

to let the sea breeze caress me. It was an invitation, I told him. Let the sea breeze in to cool you off and you'd make friends with the sea.

'That sounds so corny,' he replied. 'But I get it.'

He inched closer to me on the bench we sat on.

'I just moved here,' he said. 'This is the only thing I can do. My parents won't let me leave the island.'

'Sounds like a pretty sweet deal,' I said. 'I mean, you don't have to work…'

'But I want to,' he replied. 'What is it you do again?'

'I work in an office.' I don't remember, actually, what I did, now that I remember. 'Paperwork.'

'You want a hamburger?' he said. 'Like, we should get out of here. I'm hungry.'

We walked up the promenade until we found the little walk-up window that only served hamburgers to the tourists. It was the only hamburger stand in town. The burgers were cheap and badly made. I watched him eat three, licking the mustard from his fingers. I paid for the burgers and the large Mexican coke that he insisted on having.

I mentioned that I liked to write and he replied that he had once read Hemingway in high school and found him interesting. He mentioned that once, he'd put together poems for girls he liked, that they were all bad poems, that they made no sense.

'So like, it's obvious, I have friends, right,' he began. 'But like, I can't see them right now because I'm grounded.'

Grounded for what, I asked.

'Oh, it doesn't matter, I guess,' he replied. 'I got caught out past my curfew. Drinking with a few girls I know. And I know that sounds stupid. But I still have a curfew.'

That hour descended on us in which all beaches look like heaven—the hour prior to sunset. We walked on the shore until the cold clammy air returned from the sea and it became too unsafe to watch the surf from the jetties.

He pulled on a poncho and we sat on the damp sand, watching the moon rise.

'You seem so nice,' he said. 'And you write, which is cool...'

'You've been watching me write.'

'Who are you writing to?'

'My mom,' I replied. 'She lives alone on the mainland.'

'That seems like a nice thing to do.'

I said nothing and watched his eyes drift from mine to my chest. He ran a finger through my pecs and over the gold chain dangling from my neck. I felt the warmth of his fingers in the cleft of my pecs, as if he was drawing a ray of sunlight over my chest, gently. He undid the buttons on my guayabera and unfolded the flaps of fabric. I smiled and guided my hand over his down, embarrassed and excited by his curiosity in what had been something so ordinary. He ran a hand over mine and grabbed a fistful of my right pectoral muscle.

I recoiled.

'You have such a great tan,' he said, shrugging off a giggle. 'Do you sit out in the sun a lot?'

I ignored the question. It was a boilerplate phrase, you see. I knew why we'd been both averting our glances at one another all those days under the pergola.

'Let me feel you,' he whispered. 'Your skin is warm.'

Solitudes

He rolled over me and pressed his warm lips to mine. He kissed me deeply. He stuck his tongue in my mouth and rolled it all around. At once I tasted the sea salt that had hovered on his tanned skin all day. He pushed me onto the sand and straddled my body, and ran his hands through my hair. I felt the velvet of his mouth run over my neck. I opened my eyes and the stars had come out.

It was while I was kissing him that I remembered that I had forgotten to ask his name.

Car lights swept over the wet sand. I don't know who it would have been, but the instinct to hide him away was coming on to me.

'Let's get out of here,' I said.

I took his hand and walked us back to my tiny apartment at the edge of the promenade. It was a squat, fat little whitewashed building full of retirees. The noise of someone's radio broadcasting the late-night nautical forecast and the sound of the warm night breeze rustling the palm fronds blurred the sensations my body felt. An old woman leered at us walking up the stuccoed, recessed entrance of the building as she watered her spider lilies on her first-floor balcony. She stared down at us leerily before sliding the sliding glass door.

Sereno

We made love with the bedside lamps on. The room, I remember, was low, with a popcorn texture ceiling that was mostly asbestos and yellowed by neglect and cigarette smoke. There was a borrowed credenza from a professor friend and a turntable and the bed we made love on was ancient and immobile and impossible to keep a fitted sheet on. So when we assembled ourselves in the obscene ways we did—when we had jettisoned what we thought we were doing in favor of whatever was comfortable—the mattress buckled and lumped, the bedsheets defied our bodies, and our sweat soaked the tattered, faded floral pattern. Outside the tide swelled and deposited on the stinking shore a myriad of sargasso clumps, a dead army of invading yellow slime, in amongst the trash people had forgotten to take home with them. The sea breeze billowed the white curtains of the drawn sliding glass door that overlooked my empty stretch of promenade, lit up in hot pink light and swarming with sand flies. I kissed him, again and again, as if by kissing him I was receiving the nourishment by tiny spoonfuls, as if I was a man being nursed back to health, confident I'd never eat the same way ever again.

We showered. I fed him afterward, black beans and white rice. My mother's recipe.

He calmly washed the mauve bowl in the sink and

put it away in the rack.

'You don't have a boyfriend?'

'No,' I replied. 'Don't want one.' I lit a joint and exhaled the smoke in a slow trickle that wafted through the yellowed light of the lampshade. 'Don't get me wrong, I love being in love with someone. I just can't right now.'

'How long had you seen me out there?' he said.

I inhaled again. 'A couple of weeks. It wasn't anything intentional; I'm not a pervert or anything.'

He chuckled. 'I didn't think you were.'

He came back to the bed and sat cross-legged and took the joint from my fingers.

'I never figured you did this. I thought you...'

'Oh, don't say that, please,' I replied. 'I like weed just as much as the next person, I guess, and if you worked where I do you'd want to smoke it all the time.'

He passed the joint back to me and put his brown lips on mine. I closed my eyes and let him slip his tongue into my mouth and for a moment, time and sound blurred as it had when we climaxed together, muffled.

'So. Talk to me,' the boy said, red-eyed and stoned out of his mind. 'Do you like sports?'

I chuckled. 'No,' I said. 'I mean I'll watch them if someone invites me. But no, I'm not interested in them.'

He hit the joint again and shook his head and laughed it off.

'Is that a question you ask girls?' I said.

'No,' he said, regaining his composure. 'If I wanted to talk to a girl,' he said, tossing a strand of wet hair back, 'I'd just ask what she likes to eat.'

'Interesting. Best way to a girl's heart is through her stomach, right?'

'No,' he said. 'You gotta buy girls shit. Not just food. Like, it has to mean something.'

He stopped speaking and I felt the warm bar of his arm embrace me. He sucked on the joint one last time and hacked out a bitter cough, before finally reaching over to the ashtray to dash it out.

I opened my eyes and he was staring at me, moving back curls of my hair that had fallen over my forehead.

'I'll stay if you want,' he said, gently.

Solitudes

'I would like that,' I said.

We fell asleep looking into each other's eyes. An hour later I woke up groggy and sore-throated. The nightstand clock buzzed a dull red 11:45 and already I felt a tug to fan the weed smoke out of my apartment before my landlady would come bounding down the stairs to ask what was going on.

'You still hungry? I got a hankering for some tacos at the end of the boardwalk.'

The mythical taco cart that existed at the end of the island was one that existed in a paradox of time and space: it was either always open or always closed. And the walk there was seemingly longer than any other walk I had taken that summer. Only the junkies stuck around this late on the boardwalk to watch the tide wash away another blasted evening of their wrecked lives—and I did not want to relinquish this boy who came to me, who had smoked the last of my good weed and eaten my mother's rice and beans.

I bought a Mexican coke and he ate another couple of tacos under the cart's offensive yellow lights which crawled with chinches and blister beetles. The breeze slackened; soon there were no sand eddies whirling under the lights of the promenade. Out of nowhere came the thick raw smell of palm pith when the night rain has moistened it; that smell of naked nocturnal humidity you only smell on the hottest nights inland. When we made out in the dark parking lot behind the cart, I felt the sting of the hot sauce he had put on his tacos and the taste of pickled jalapeño, which numbed my lips and made me crave the taste of tequila slaked with lime. When he kissed me I felt weak-kneed and suddenly awkward, and I had suddenly reverted to seventeen and a half with the overwrought French novel I'd been reading suddenly falling out of my hands, to watch the star quarterback say hello to me in passing.

I walked him back to the palatial house in pink stucco that he called home. The sand had settled and the stars had come out on this dark limb of the island. We walked holding hands and looking up to see if we recognized constellations, but the haze of the weed and our lust made that impossible.

He gently unlatched a wrought iron gate and kissed me through the bars.

'Will I see you tomorrow?' I asked him.

'Yes. Maybe. I'll see if I can find you,' he replied.

'I wasn't expecting this at all,' I said.

He shrugged and I heard him chortle. I thought, lucky me, this errant boy of sand and water, who had come to me, kissed me, lay naked with me in my bed, eaten from my refrigerator, used up the last twenty in my wallet until payday.

'Come and see me tomorrow,' I said, passing him my business card through the bars of the gate. He pocketed the card quickly.

'I have to go now,' he said. He ascended the pavers and disappeared behind the corner of the pink stucco house.

I was late for work the next day, and ran into the full glare of the hot sun with my white shirt half buttoned and my sandals in my hands. I ran down the promenade feeling the full weight of the night on my shoulders and the hot sand of the walk roasting the bare soles of my feet. With each footfall I imagined he was waiting for me at the pergola as the high tide roared inland. I passed the square and looked left to see the pergola beset with balloons and children; the grey-green lip of the sea had bitten into the brown sand just a few hundred yards and a gaggle of children chased the pipers with sticks.

Sereno

Someone was having a birthday party on the beach. I'd have to eat lunch at my desk again.

I arrived at the pink stuccoed building with the half-basement, walked downstairs to where the office was, and dressed at the front door. No one inside noticed me slamming my brown sandals on the concrete and practically walking into them. I opened the door and immediately felt the heavy rush of the air conditioning cool my sweaty brow.

'Sorry I'm late,' I said to the oblivious secretary, whose brown, gold-bangled arms rifled through an immense file. She did not look up as I rushed toward my own little mountain of paper.

The secretary cleared her throat and slapped the file down on her desk and pulled another one out of the file. 'The Deakins account is past due again, naturally,' she said, sipping from an immense coffee cup. 'We should send a form letter.'

'I can get one faxed over to the mainland.'

'Do you think you can catch a bus over there? Deakins lives off of the bay. You can't miss it, it's right off the bridge. I can hold down the phones.'

'Are you serious? Is it that bad?' I asked.

Solitudes

'Think of it as a little errand. I'll let you use your lunch period to get back so you won't be late, either,' the secretary replied.

Twenty minutes later I stood fanning myself sitting on a bench in the shade of a hot pink bougainvillea awaiting the shuttle bus to the mainland that took the aged and infirm across the nameless concrete bridge to the grocery store.

An old man sitting next to me placed his hand on his wife's thigh. 'Did you say twenty minutes?'

'Yes. No. I don't know actually,' the wife replied.

The glare from the sea was relentless.

I hastily dropped off the form letter and the file in the mailbox at Deakins' houseboat. No one was home. I looked back toward the island and saw an immense grey arc of clouds forming on the high sea. The sea breeze was coming in. I had to get back to the bus stop quickly if I wanted to avoid the rain. So I ran again—back up the dock and towards the street teeming with summer tourist traffic—and found the bus arriving just as I got there. I hopped on and found it packed with half-naked splotchy-skinned old people fanning themselves with copies of the Island Penny Saver.

Sereno

'Bus is full,' the bus driver replied. 'You can if you want wait. Next bus come in twenty, OK?'

I stepped off the bus and began walking toward the bridge. I walked diligently, ignoring the cars full of children gawking at me. I didn't care. I had to get back to the office to see him.

When I did, the secretary laughed at me. I'd been thoroughly soaked by the afternoon downpour.

'You're lucky you didn't get that file wet; the boss would have killed you if that happened,' she said with a chuckle. She sat down and looked at her piles of paper and did not look up at me again.

'By the way,' she said, 'someone came to see you while you were out.'

Bromeliads and rain are my constant companions in this place. The rain soaks the pavers of the apartment building I live in now, which has a Spanish courtyard with monsteras and the occasional large spider. Skinks run through the potted gardenias. It rains here all the time. I think of my time on the island, and I think of that boy.

Solitudes

I kept on waiting for him to show up for three months. He never did. I didn't know that his parents had abruptly left the island because the tourist season was coming to an end—never mind that I didn't think he was a tourist—no one that perfect can't not be. My own season was coming to a close on the island. I held that job for another three months before the company moved operations off the island. I already was high and dry in that island town; I might as well have just sat there at the pergola until the unemployment checks ran out. Maybe, I surmised, he was just playing hard to get. One evening I walked to the end of the promenade and stood there at the gate in front of his house, waited for him to part the curtains. But the house was empty, shuttered; the hurricane that came afterward blew everything off that side of the island and only prickly pears and palmettos grow there now.

On my last night in town I resolved to wait for him. I descended from the promenade and sat at the picnic table under the pergola in the dark all evening, waving sand flies off of my bare feet. I thought I saw him around ten-thirty, accompanied by a girl, and in the dark under the pergola I watched him try and fail at making her kiss him. My heart beat out of my chest. My palms got sweaty and I nervously wiped them on my sad white bermuda shorts there in the dark. After a few minutes of ill-conceived heavy petting the girl left, disgusted and frustrated. The fiasco was by this time evident. I watched him in the starless dark as he walked toward the sea, his gait so identical to that boy's, the silhouette of his body a sharp thin profile against the salty dark of the ocean. And in that moment, I wanted to arrest time to wander to him to see if it was really him—to know his body, to see his face, to ask him what he'd been thinking of. In that moment, I wondered if once, after that dangerous and incipient moment when he'd kissed me on the beach, whether he'd thought of me, whether he said my name while in the shower or while alone in bed; if he had longed for my body the way I had longed for his. In the solitude of the present, I sit with this moment: the carefree young man and the aloof ancient ocean, his big wide shoulders and the great unknowing sea, meeting one another along the desolate margins of the shore, to stare at one another like lovers who know nothing of their love for one another.

Sereno

Roundhay Garden Scene

THE APPARATUS—*the receiver,* AS LOUIS called it—was an awkward box of oak dovetailed together and fitted with scrap brass. Louis had no name for it other than *the receiver.* All the vibrancy of the world would pass silently through three lenses—maybe six, maybe eight or nine, maybe sixteen—transmuted upside-down and backward through the glimmer of soft convex and concave lenses, translated into silent witnessing onto scraps of paper, extracted in the dark and printed on a sheet of gelatin. Roses, scraps of fabric, fine wooden veneers, scents, smells, the feel of English brick pavers and the faces of freckled schoolboys, fog, water, people. It was more than a camera, Louis said to his friends, to anyone who would listen to him: it was a mechanism to record forever the very act of living.

Throughout that marvelous year of 1888 Louis worked day and night on the apparatus. He refined the lenses, polished and reworked the mechanism and the frame, endlessly threw himself into the complex mathematical and chemical precision of the photographer's world. Everyone worried for him: his wife Elizabeth, his son Adolphe, his in-laws, the Whitleys. At dinner he railed against the injustice of the patent bureaucracy and how unbearably *long* the process had been. The spring and summer had come and gone and Louis had what he wanted: an American patent and time. In the meantime he photographed everything that moved: butterflies hovering over flowers in the garden, the rustling of birds in the trees, stiff-necked coachmen steering broughams down the road, his son playing his brother's old concertina. But something always happened: the glass plates would shatter, the emulsion would spoil, a rare subject just always darting away into the bright blue world to avoid being captured by the magic device. No one could stop Louis Le Prince. He was doing what he loved to do.

This autumn had been slow to settle in, and the afternoons were filled with that gorgeous low-angled light that painters like him coveted like delicious sin. When Louis wasn't tinkering, he was drawing, painting, watching his boy grow into a man, kissing his wife delicately in the tender purple evenings, watching his mother-in-law Sarah blow out candle in the dining room, relishing the hearty, pipe tobacco-stained laugh of his elderly father-in-law Joseph. He counted himself lucky: Elizabeth was the most beautiful woman in his world, and Adolphe was smart and agile, a boy who could conquer the world. The Whitleys were indulgent with him, unlike his very French parents who had practically abandoned him to the great Daguerre. His life was a world of lavender pique and great passing clouds, a world of tender flaxen hills dotted with poppies in France and the grey mists of autumnal London with its smell of horse dung and samphire, a caress of terry cloth and soft white flowers, the lacey, brilliant white days of summer with its heart-blood stain of chilled Burgundy wine, a time of endless vernissage and finissage.

And now the apparatus sat in its mysterious box, waiting to be summoned. The American addendum to the patent had been filed, accepted; all he had to do was make an impression, demonstrate nothing less than a miracle. At first there were sixteen eyes in the apparatus, then nine; what had worked was three, but he had settled in this case for one. So many eyes in which to apprehend the beauty of the world: an Argus of oakwood, a golem of brass, sitting silently like a many-eyed spider in its case lined with velveteen and smelling of spirit of nitre. When Louis held it in his hands at the workshop it felt heavier than newborn Adolphe, heavier than a Leeds brick, heavier than a plate of roast with new potatoes and a Yorkshire pudding. They'd be crossing the Atlantic in a steam ship soon, him and Lizzie and Adolphe, off to conquer America again, to dazzle its spectators and capture on that flimsy paper film all those moribund Indians and grizzled old cowboys and wide-smiling minstrels, the spoils of an empire in the golden west.

'Papa,' Adolphe called from upstairs. 'I can't find my shoes.'

The house on Park Square that Louis lived in was modest. But he relished the light passing through a copse of hawthorns in the afternoon on days like these, filtering through the tall windows. Such perfect writing weather. He looked under his writing desk and found Adolphe's shoes.

'They are where you always leave them, *mon fils.*'

Down the stairs bounded sixteen year old Adolphe, lanky, scrubbed, rosy-cheeked, in ill-fitting brown trousers that used to dip below his ankles before the growth spurt.

'And you will be very wise not to leave them downstairs again.'

'I'm sorry,' Adolphe said. Leeds had been growing on him, his accent changing to fit the clipped Yorkshire of his mates in school. 'I got lost reading that novel upstairs.'

'Help me to move the apparatus to the carriage, *mon fils.*'

'You're not planning to bring that with you, are you, Monsieur?' Lizzie said, walking into the room. She straightened out her day dress. 'Mummy said she really wants to keep any discussion about cameras out of the house.'

Louis got up and placed his big, bare hands on her tiny shoulders and rubbed them gently.

Roundhay Garden Scene

'I promise I won't bring up anything too boring at dinner. They're tired of my prattle.'

'It's not that,' Lizzie replied. 'Mamma is not feeling well. The discussion of money is not conducive to her health or wellbeing in the slightest. I am sure she will be happy to hear of your progress.'

'She very well should be,' Louis replied. 'Oh, how I would love to take Mamma and Papa to America with us,' he said, his voice swelling with optimism. He embraced her and she could smell of the sharp note of the snuff he had just pinched. 'Wouldn't that be gay? To show them New York City. Philadelphia. Perhaps even California. The good air would clear her lungs.'

'Be realistic, Louis. We should take a rail trip, if possible. Your brother in Dijon? Your mother?'

'It has been a long time,' Louis said, gently. He looked down at her with his great grey eyes, eyes that relayed tenderness and strength in one look. 'I suppose we can investigate the matter later, if you wish. It would be good for all of us once this patent business is done.'

She smiled and kissed him under the shade of her parasol.

The clock struck four o'clock. Adolphe carefully loaded the apparatus in the back of his father's buckboard, helped his mother in, and they set off at a slow clop towards Roundhay Cottage.

Roundhay was magical. A place truly preserved from time and sadness. The Whitleys lived comfortably, but not extravagantly. They had a maid, Marie, who could do Yorkshire and French cooking. But what Louis loved about Roundhay was its solitude, its dew-drop stillness, its enclosure of privet and fallen leaves. There could be no tragedy there.

Louis found his mother-in-law Sarah Whitley leaning on her cane, squinting into the golden sunset outside of Roundhay Cottage when they arrived.

'How did you manage?' she said. 'No great delays?'

'None,' Lizzie said, stepping off. 'A perfectly quiet afternoon.'

Adolphe jumped off the buckboard.

'Hello there, boy,' Sarah said, embracing Adolphe.

Adolphe planted two kisses on her cheeks. She stood there looking at her lanky giant with his scuzzy beard.

'Papa has brought *the apparatus* over,' he said. 'He wants to take some photographs in the garden.'

Roundhay Garden Scene

'I see,' Sarah replied, a note of concern ringing in her voice. 'But when did you want to do it, dear?'

'*Belle-mère*,' Louis said, embracing Sarah and kissing her on both cheeks. 'Sunday, with your permission, of course. I am aware of our little agreement. I couldn't resist. I want to make a family portrait.'

'I'm rather bemused by the request,' Sarah replied, a little overwhelmed. 'But do come in.'

Before dinner was served, Adolphe, who'd been learning to play the harmonium, played a song by Meyerbeer. Louis, feeling the lilt in his glass of madeira, sang a catch of the stuffy old tune. Sarah loved to hear him sing, especially in French. Lizzie loved watching him and Joseph play kipper and drink whiskey together, father and would-be son and beautiful boy who couldn't put down terribly interesting, terribly lurid books, all sitting there before a roaring and generously warm fire like a trio of Russian generals.

Louis had never been happier. The apparatus would lift the cloud of uncertainty and doubt from the world they lived in—no more outrageous bills, no more worries about how'd they'd manage America—nothing. No more quibbling with brother John over money just to get by. Everything solved: Adolphe at Oxford reading the classics, summers in the Rhône or at Baden-Baden, just like in the sentimental novels she'd read as as a girl. A house in Paris and dresses from Worth. Deep down, Lizzie had wanted to dress up for the opera, to wear a dress the color of midnight and to drink maraschino punch and to ride, white-gloved and smelling of roses, with Louis to the Opéra Garnier, with everyone looking on them. Yes, her, they'd say. That's Louis Le Prince's wife. Madame Le Prince.

There was a knock at the door.

Sarah put down her cup of tea. 'Our surprise guest.'

Marie went to the door and opened it.

A passing rain shower had appeared over the tops of the trees and in the twilight appeared as a brilliant tower of pink flame. The rain it brought came on rather suddenly and pattered on the alder trees with such intensity that it sounded like a flight of pigeons.

'Good evening, Miss Hartley,' Marie said.

It was a cold, October rain and the rain-soaked air crept low on the parqueted floor of the foyer and into the parlor. Miss Hartley stepped in, handed her coat and umbrella to Marie, and strode into the shaft of warm firelight emerging from the parlor.

'Anne!' Lizzie said. 'But we weren't expecting you *at all*.'

Anne Hartley was an old school friend of Lizzie.

Roundhay Garden Scene

The formerly gangly girl who had timidly followed Lizzie around everywhere had blossomed into a rather mysterious-looking woman. She lived just down the street in her late parents' home, and taught art to the wealthy girls that occasionally traveled into Leeds to escape dreary, tired old London. Sometimes she came over to look after Joseph and Sarah. Whereas Lizzie had escaped Leeds with her Bohemian husband and his revolving carousel of daguerrotypes and painted pots, Anne stayed close to home, cultivated flowers, taught watercolor, dressed in deep violet, wore an onyx ring. A queen of the night, if there ever was one.

'I'm not too late, am I?' Anne said.

'Not at all,' Lizzie said, rising to embrace her.

Louis had been at the fireplace lighting his pipe when Anne walked in. Like Lizzie, she had a certain air that she brought with her everywhere she went. It was unmistakeable. He could smell the rain lingering on Anne's shoulders, the smell of oak, moss and wet earth. The hearty smell of England.

Their eyes met. Anne's eyes bore such a strange violet-green light in them, an alexandrite on watered black damask. He at once remembered a boating trip they'd taken years ago, when his muttonchops were not as long and his bright eyes sparkled like the grey-blue water all around them.

'Miss Hartley,' he said, and kissed her hand. She wasn't used to such French excesses of form. Englishmen didn't have that sort of *savoir-vivre*. Maybe that was why she had missed him so much.

'Mrs Whitley had asked me to come, to celebrate your achievement—I thought it would be most appropriate to at least present myself for dinner.'

'What a surprise indeed. The last we saw of you was before you left. For America. St Louis, I believe,' Lizzie interjected.

'Ah yes,' Louis replied, suddenly remembering the sound of summer cicadas and the bracing heat of summer. 'A ghastly time, if I remember. No money, and me and John practically begging in the streets for anyone to come and see our exhibit... I can't remember the name now.'

'*The Siege of Vicksburg*,' Lizzie said. 'We were told they'd be unsympathetic there. But they loved his paintings. Very much like Manet's, we were told.'

Louis let her talk, let her drop the embarrassing bits out. Louis let her have her little digs. Anne nodded politely, never taking her eyes off Louis'.

'To be back *here*,' Anne said. 'Do you remember when we were younger, Elizabeth? Eating cherries in the summer, and going boating with the other girls? The summer that John returned with Louis from Leipzig.'

'I can't forget at all,' Lizzie replied.

'I painted your portrait in oils that year,' Louis replied, closing his eyes and letting his memory lean into the warm, summery haze of the past. He inhaled her scent of violets and woodruff, remembered Anne's dark hair contrasting with with the white linen dress stained with strawberry juice.

'One of many,' Anne replied. 'Those were perfectly lovely days.'

He knew she felt the same June warmth. It was a different feeling than merely standing by the fire. When Anne breathed he felt the branches of trees move in the wind, a sensation he had only felt with Lizzie.

'It isn't that I have reservations to this newest project, Louis. You must understand that.'

Joseph knocked back his tiny liqueur glass and puffed on his pipe.

'I rather like the idea of using Whitley brass. My overall concern is for your family. The last few endeavors we have had have met with...'

'Of course I understand, beau-père.'

'I have never doubted your abilities in the slightest. The financial cost alone—that is what concerns me, you see.'

'The school is doing well, *beau-père*. Lizzie and myself are taking on new students in painting and pottery almost all the time. The retention rates are high. Our recent successes with the portraits of the Queen and Lord Gladstone have secured our happiness, if not just for a little while.'

Joseph momentarily relaxed in the green chair he usually sat in before dinner.

'I'm afraid Whitley Partners can't take another bad hit like we had when John managed it. The constant traveling up and down the Continent, worthless expansion without any forethought as to permanency...and of course the familial impact that such endeavors have.'

Joseph caught a dry breath and tried to keep his frustration with his eldest son from showing. Louis reached across the table and took Joseph's hand. Like a real son would have done.

'I know you are worried for my success, *mon papa*. I promise this apparatus will elevate all of our fortunes.'

'If you go to America,' Joseph said, 'you must be shewd.

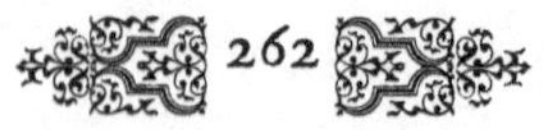

Roundhay Garden Scene

It's a great world out there; it would be a shame if this achievement were to fly out of your hands altogether.'

The clock in the hall struck seven and its chimes stirred something in Louis. Sarah couldn't set the table anymore, and with Marie busy in the kitchen, Lizzie and Adolphe and Louis set out the Whitley china. Only Sarah stayed in the parlor to sip her tea and to count her losses: her eldest son absconded to the Continent, an exile in name only, the son-in-law now decamping for America, and the world becoming uneasier with the passage of the days. She had been more or less ill for ten years. Everything ached. It was hard to breathe. Nothing made sense anymore. Once familiar tasks like setting a table seemed so monstrous now, those things that once were obligatory displays of love, of togetherness. When dinnertime came Sarah insisted in bringing out the roast and let Joseph cut it, even though his arthritis usually prevented him from doing so. Joseph demurred, so he let Louis do it. What John could not do, Louis had done. He felt oddly unsure about this arrangement of family responsibility. Families didn't make sense to Louis and yet he was able to have one. He wrote his mother twice monthly in long letters that tended to avoid the past and barely mention the present, and her replies were terse and full of general advice. *You must pray everyday. Do not bathe in cold water in September. The Americans are bad because I once knew one. The government is full of anticlericals and Masons. I wish you had*

not moved to such a cold climate. What is your general opinion of espaliering a cherry tree?

And yet dinner with the Whitleys was convivial. Friends like Anne were blessings, if only because Lizzie had taken him out of the painter's smock and into salons with old college friends who painted birds in their leisure time and were now married to bankers. Wine spilled freely from crystal flacons. There were *marrons glacés*, trifles, chocolates, soirées, an occasional trip to Spa, a sighting of Richard and Cosima Wagner on their way to Bayreuth...

'I cannot tell you how many times I have thought about seeing you again,' Anne said to Louis in the study after dinner. 'It is very good to see you. I have missed you so.'

He wasn't looking at her. He was looking at the arms of the mantle clock creep toward ten. Anne Hartley, the beautiful and mysterious friend, had loved Louis, maybe still did. Louis wanted to reciprocate her joy at seeing him, but he stifled the feelings bubbling up inside of him like the madeira he'd had too much of.

'You are very kind, if not but a little shocking. I thought you had forgotten about me.'

'Forgive me if I seem too forward.'

'You could never be that,' he said, and this time he was

looking at her.

'God did not favor me with the fortune you've had. To travel. To America! To see all that you have seen.'

'There is no such thing as a perfect world, Miss Anne. Behind all of that good luck was hard work.'

'Like I said, forgive me if seeing you does arouse in me trifling sentiments. It is beyond the pale of polite society to have them, believe me.'

Louis gently smiled and took her hands.

'We are best friends, Mademoiselle Anne. All of those times where we had lunched and boated or sung silly songs—those times are all within reach. Just because I have not been present here in Leeds to pay a visit does not mean my sentiments have abated in any way.'

Anne blushed, and the words tangled themselves in her brain, forbidding a response.

'I do love Lizzie. But when we were in St Louis for the Exposition,' he whispered, letting his guard down, 'I could not help but think about you.'

The *sôle meunière* and the roast sank in his entrails

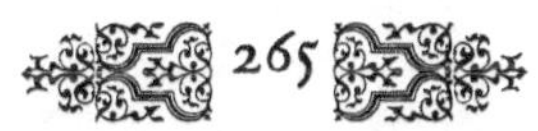

like a brick thrown down a deep well. His thoughts were seized with emulsions, with glass plates shattering in the starless black of his mind, with endless smudgy fingerprints of silver-gray and corroded paper drifting like black ashes into his dreamworld. He sat before the fire and let it speak to him, thought of Lizzie baring her breasts and kissing him and Anne under the cork-oak of some nameless place in Sodom and imagined that the apparatus had captured it all. Maybe it had: maybe he had taken a picture of them together, looking still and emotionless, like a Delacroix. *A Still Life of Two Women Kissing.* Liberty leading the inventor. Wouldn't *that* be some painting by Delacroix? Only this time, the great glass-eyed box would be witness to their sin.

Lizzie sat on the bed in the guest room, pulled off her stockings and wiggled her toes.

'Don't think I didn't hear you and Anne in the study.'

The hairs on the back of Louis' head rose.

'I'm not upset, you know. I know she fancies you a great deal.'

He turned his head back toward her.

'You're not?'

'No, I'm not,' Lizzie replied. 'Anne has always been a

great fool when it comes to men. She's always been overtly inclined to be sentimental. I can forgive sentimentality if it's a defect of the mind.'

'I am sentimental, too. Perhaps I am mad.'

'That's because you're *French*, my love,' she replied with a giggle. Lizzie, his libertine wife. 'I feel almost sorry for her. Never married. Or rather, would have been married. If John had summoned up the courage to petition her hand.'

'You are forgetting, husband, that she never liked John. She didn't care for his body. Ah, yes. Her mother was very much against the match as well, if I recall.'

'That's right,' Lizzie said, giggling. 'She always liked the athletic boys. Now, come away from the fire, dear husband. Come away from the fire and lay down with me.'

Sarah at Saturday breakfast, a swoop of chartreuse green and black, holding a bouquet of dying marigolds, in the white-tiled kitchen, where only Marie ventured to go: 'But you must understand, my dear. My constitution is much improved.'

'But *belle-mère*, your cough,' Louis said. 'Going out to the grocer's this morning won't do you any good.'

'Nonsense,' Sarah replied. 'Marie will go with me as she did during the summer. Won't you?'

'I will, ma'am,' Marie replied.

'Perhaps Adolphe can go with you.'

'I agree that would be most helpful. Adolphe, wouldn't you like to go to the market with *grand-mère*?'

'Papa said I have to help him set up in the garden.'

'It's true,' Louis replied, feeling a little helpless. 'If you need another companion, however, Adolphe will go with you.'

'But I do not think any of you *understand*. I am feeling stronger than I have felt in many months. I daresay I may be able to attend evensong this evening with Mr Whitley.'

'Have you had a look at the weather glass this morning?' Lizzie put her coffee cup down. 'I saw frost on the leaves.'

'It is *nothing*, I assure you,' Sarah said, rasping. 'The sun will be coming out soon. I will be fine. Marie: once you're finished with the washing up, help me to attire, won't you?'

And like that she retreated, regal and unconquered.

'*Go* with her,' Louis said to Lizzie.

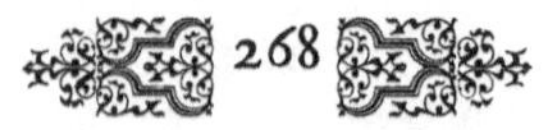

Roundhay Garden Scene

By ten, Louis had spread out on the table in the study his notes, his schematics, long black lines of rapidly fading ink that sketched out the apparatus, the winding mechanism to capture life flitting before the silent glass lenses. The room felt hot and stifling, as if summer had clung to the rafters and only collapsed onto Louis' shoulders the moment he walked in after breakfast.

He had not slept well: at 3 AM he was woken by a terrible nightmare. Lizzie crying, the room spinning, the world fading in a haze of white smoke amidst the smell of birdshot and hot iron. He did not know where he was but there were creditors, fat and short and stout and angry, waiting at the Gare St-Lazare with the police and George Eastman, a madman in a Confederate uniform, his hands full of rolls of crushed paper film. The apparatus grew and grew until it had sprouted tentacles of hissing electrified wire and crept up the wall like a large, threatening spider.

He undid himself from Lizzie's embrace and the soporific warmth of the guest room and walked downstairs into the study. He stood in the still dark of 4 AM and watched a meteor streak into oblivion, a single silver-green thread against a blue-black canvas of sky. Imagine what it would be like to remember this moment, to relive it! A frisson of wonder and excitement shivered down his spine like a pebble cascading down a silken tube.

If his calculations were still correct, 12 frames

could be produced on one roll of paper film. The resulting impressions would be fleeting; just a few seconds. If accomplished, however, the results would be self-evident. Only if Mr Eastman would let him have as much of the fragile paper film... he had been so generous and so kind in his last few letters...

There was a knock at the door.

'Don't bother me,' Louis said.

'It is only me,' Anne said from behind the door. Her heard the rustle of her bustle, the *chi-chi* of her taffeta petticoats passing the threshold.

'Have some tea, Monsieur.'

'You are too kind.'

For a moment he imagined Anne wearing one of Lizzie's old dresses, a deep blue velvet evening gown she wore to someone's forgotten house party. Anne's body in Lizzie's dress... the women identical to one another... he could undo the laces and the skin would be the same... the same scent of muriatic bath, milled soap, violets...

He went to the door and opened it.

Woman with a tea set. She was in a black dress, not a blue one. She had a pocket watch, a set of pince-nez glasses, a tiny white cameo. The Saturday morning light caught the grey in her eyes and in the individual strands of her chestnut hair, so few. Little silver threads of worry and doubt.

'You didn't have to, Anne.' Louis said.

'It's almost eleven, anyway,' she said, gliding in. 'Where shall I set it?'

Louis went back to the table and scuttled the plans away.

'Here, *ma chère*,' he said. 'You are very kind.'

'Be reasonable, Louis,' she said. 'You look spectral. You must not overexert yourself—'

'Oh, mademoiselle Anne, if you only knew. Perhaps I *am* overexerting myself.'

'It's such a fine morning, too. Really one of the best I've seen.'

She poured him a cup of tea. She knew how he took his tea—had seen him in times past, so reverently and reservedly slip a small bit of clotted cream into the tiny cup, the usual soupçon of sugar. It was a British custom he had never really grown accustomed to: elevenses, tea with lady friends.

Sereno

He drank the tea slowly, watched the sparrows leap from branch to branch on the privet outside in the garden.

'This afternoon I will commence my experiment in the gardens. I will take some exposures and calibrate the lenses on the apparatus.'

'Is that why you've been here in the library? Planning?'

Louis sensed an ulterior motive in her question.

'I wanted to be alone... I keep on making a mathematical error which I feel will affect the rate of... Forget I said anything, Anne. You must find such discussions absolutely abominable; they are not suitable for discussion with ladies. Nor am I very good company when I am in this state, I am afraid.'

'I don't find them abominable at all, on the contrary... Louis, that is one thing you may have never understood about me. I've always been interested in the scientific things you do.'

They garden they looked out sparkled with dew, rustled with the sound of the drab wings of sparrows fluttering among the red bare branches of privet.

'The only reason I have invested so much time into the apparatus is for money,' he said. 'For Lizzie and Adolphe, for the future of Whitley Brass.'

Roundhay Garden Scene

'You don't strike me as someone who is bad with money, Louis.'

'On the contrary, I am, Anne. Very bad. Only Lizzie helps to keep us afloat. And her parents have been very generous. If it were not for them I'd be a great failure.'

'You are no failure, Louis. Not in my estimation. Quite the contrary.'

'You think so?'

'I know so,' Anne said. 'I have always admired your brilliance. And for all the things that have taken place in your life, you deserve all of the recognition.'

Her voice soothed the sting of anxiety inside him.

'I suppose we really didn't catch up last night at all, with dinner and all. Tell me, Anne: how is your painting school? Your girls?'

She was taken back by this interrogation. 'My *girls*? You mean the girls I teach manners to?'

Louis nodded.

'I suppose they're fine,' she replied. 'Obviously my luck in obtaining girls who wish to be educated is rather lacking here in Leeds, but that is another story. And of course you know that I watercolor all the time.'

'Ah, is that so?'

'Of course,' she said, lowering her voice to a whisper, as if she were relaying a dirty secret. 'I only paint when I feel inspired to. For example, the sunsets, or when I read a poem, or finish a novel.'

'We are both terribly sentimental beings,' Louis said, with a resignation. 'Quite like a curse.'

'I wouldn't say that,' Anne replied.

He watched Anne take up the tea tray and head down the hall. The sunlight filtering through the tall windows had made the encounter feel stuffy and inartificial. He could have swept her up and stripped her bare and bitten into the raw white flesh of her sweet smelling breasts and she would not have cared. He could tell by the way she had positioned her body that she wanted to be close to him, but could not bring herself to the moment. Instead all they had was half-cold tea and clots of cream and toast points and middling strawberry jam. They had agreed to tea at four with Lizzie and Adolphe, the apparatus an obligatory stone guest. He suppressed those Don Giovanni feelings as he resumed his calculations focused on the hand-crank, his desire twisting silently into the dull brassy box that held the glass eye.

Roundhay Garden Scene

The eye awakened under a grey-green fog, and then two figures came into view, curling from right to left around the curve of the lens. Louis twisted a ring and he could see a familiar grey muslin shawl, the warm tone of a white-gloved hand closing a parasol.

'Do you think you'll miss the old world very much before traveling to America?'

'No. I imagine it'll take some getting used to. Of course I'll miss France, the Norman countryside…Paris, of course. I suppose if all works out well we'll have another house in France we can summer in. I heard that in New York it's all the rage to have a summer house in France.'

'It seems to be the custom in America to brag about the size and locations of one's summer houses,' he heard Sarah say. 'A rather odd pastime.'

Louis tweaked a brass ring and the cloudy figures came into view, hovering upside down in the fuzzy eye of the camera. A light rain had broken up just long enough for the sun to emerge in time for the afternoon tea. It was still warm enough to take it on the terrace in the garden, perhaps the last time to do so.

'Of course, it really is rather remarkable to travel to America in the first place. Such a wild, undiscovered place. A paradise, really.'

'Now that is something that strains credibility,' Sarah replied.

Even under the glass eye the china teapot had an otherworldly luster. Louis loved the convex bubble world of the camera. The women had leaned out of the garden door and held a hand out just as the rain had finished soaking the terrace and a rainbow had formed in the east. The clock had struck four and Marie came out with the service, steam rising from the teapot like incense smoke from a thurible. It was Anne's grey muslin shawl that Louis had seen bloom from a hidden channel of violet, her white-gloved hand that closed the white bird of parasol.

The figures unfolded and rejoined from one to three, like the hidden essence of the Trinity achingly bending down to stir the waters below it. A cloud passed in front of the vision: Joseph emerging on the terrace.

'Tea time,' he said, a great brown and grey fog eclipsing Sarah and Lizzie and Anne. 'And the rain stopped, finally.'

'Do come sit down, Father,' Lizzie said.

'Louis, what are you doing there?'

'Calibrating the lens,' he replied.

'America is rather interesting. New York is comparable to any European city. When I taught at the Deaf School there I met nothing but the most kind and generous people. We were so well treated there. Weren't we, Louis?'

Louis said nothing. From the perspective of the eye the Trinity unmounted, the light changed, and suddenly a cast of golden leapt from the grey muslin cloud. Sarah poured him a cup of tea and a lush silence descended with the golden color, slanted forward into the green-grey stain of garden hedge and rough stone. They all came into view, a family cast almost in bas-relief against the great golden glow of a fading October afternoon.

'Oh, they are were all nice, I suppose. Terrible artists themselves, but fine connoisseurs. Or isn't that your general opinion, *beau-père*?'

'Don't get me involved at all in the great debate about how charming America is. What's charming is their money, and how much they're willing to spend it. I built Whitley Brass with an American investor who wanted me to make valves for him. I daresay I don't regret that decision.'

'One could say that American greed has made our family what it is.'

'But that isn't at all *true*,' Sarah replied, a laugh escaping in a few sharp gasps. 'I'd rather not think of it that way.' She shifted her bustle and set down her teacup. 'Louis darling, come away from that already. Have some tea.

The afternoon is getting quite pretty.'

'I will,' Louis said, bending down to recalibrate the lens.

The frame was set. Against the backdrop of the house with its tall windows taking in the brunt of the lowering sunlight, the quartet finally assembled, somewhat mismatched, against the grey-green leaves and the speckle of moss and freshly fallen rain. They sat there on wicker chairs brought in from the library, bustles the color of madder and wisteria, a tortoiseshell comb, a watch fob of silver, a sleek line of black beads in passementerie, a rain of onyx tears against a sea of black watered silk. A family portrait.

Louis stood straight up and rolled up his sleeves. A rumble of distant thunder bruited through the parting October sky.

Once again Louis retired the brass box, back to its veneered monstrance in the library. The rain did not come, but the cool evening air descended once more until the moors around Roundhay were cloaked in delicate veils of fog. Above, the sky changed colors: from its shower of gold and grey, to a receding scale of blues and purples, until finally the evening star emerged, singular and serene, like an angel above the house, and settled over the elms like a stud affixed to the sphere of heaven itself.

Roundhay Garden Scene

'Marie, the sunflowers,' Sarah said. 'Let's put them up in the vase when I return from evensong, shall we?'

Louis looked up from his book of sketches to see an armful of Russian sunflowers, heads as big as copper trenchers, laying on the cherry dining table, in a cradle of butcher paper.

'Yes, ma'am,' Marie replied from the kitchen.

'Mamma, please do not forget to cover yourself with your shawl before going to church this evening,' Lizzie said.

'I feel perfectly fine, dear,' she replied. In Sarah's blue eyes Louis noted a hint of disdain for the request. 'I had a perfectly good walk this morning with Adolphe. Louis, don't you like the sunflowers?'

'They're quite lovely, *belle-mère*. You must be very careful of the night air, my dear Mrs Whitley... I hope you will not tarry so long in prayer before dinner. Although I can see why one would want to be so thankful to God.'

'I had such a wonderful day. The sunflowers are quite the *pièce de resistance*, I feel,' she responded. 'Really, I had such a perfect little walk around the town. It appears that so much of the neighborhood has changed. The market no longer feels the same.' Her tone softened, became wistful. 'I had almost forgotten the color of the sky, the color of certain buildings, Louis. How had I forgotten that?'

'Mamma, you were quite sick with that awful cold,' Lizzie replied. 'That is why we have been so worried, Louis and I. Which is why I insisted that you take Adolphe with you.'

'Am I really that weak to you?' Sarah asked.

'No, but you are very precious to us,' Louis replied.

Once they had seen Sarah and Joseph off to church, Louis and Lizzie returned to the dining room. One by one, Lizzie lit the lamps and the room emerged out of the dark in piecework. Husband and wife separated the sunflowers, filled a blue ware china vase with water, sank them deep into the vase.

He caressed her face and shoulders with her hands, looked deeply into her eyes, conveyed with his own the great love he felt for her, this beautiful creature he'd captured and kept for years.

'Anne confided to me that you were feeling like a failure again.'

'She did?'

Lizzie smiled. 'She is incapable of keeping secrets

from me. She knows you all too well.' She raised her eyes up at him. 'I guess the question is, do you feel like one?'

His silence was pregnant with memories of America, with how beautiful it was... the mansions on Fifth Avenue, New York Harbor, gleaming with sparkling waves and tall ships, Newport with its extravagance and its perfect sandy beaches...

'Compared to everything we've seen in America? Yes, Lizzie. Yes, I do feel like a failure. I want to leave Leeds desperately. Not to London. Not to Paris. Certainly not any other capital in Europe. But to America. And if I had it my way I'd best Eastman for all he had, take my American patent and buy the devil out of his company. And then you'd never have to worry about money ever again.'

Her response surprised him. Her brow furrowed.

'Nothing of that concerns me, Louis,' she replied. 'The receiver may or may not change all of our fortunes. It is foolhardy to believe that it will,' she said. 'But I believe in you. And you must never, ever say that you are failure. Everything we have as a family we owe to one another.'

'As always you are right,' Louis said.

She stood on her tiptoes to kiss him gently, and he could savor the first time he'd ever kissed her, in a brougham in London, after seeing a play he'd forgotten.

'As for moving... yes, I do think it's time for a change. I did enjoy New York a great deal. There were very nice people there and I enjoyed having something smart to wear. Do you think we could ever convince Mamma to come with us?'

'I don't think she'd be able to handle a trip like that.'

'Yes, I suppose so,' Lizzie replied. 'Maybe Anne, then.'

'Anne?' Louis said. Anne who had missed out on everything? On love, on romance? Anne who knew nothing but watercolors and purple martins and rain-soaked hills?

'Yes, her, Louis. Why not? She's been a friend of ours for years. Maybe a trip to America will stoke her curiosity. Maybe she'll find some other chap who'll take a fancy to her. An American one.'

'One doesn't go about setting out beaux for one's best friends,' Louis said with a sly chuckle.

'I shall ask her tonight before bed,' Lizzie said. 'She'll say yes, just you wait.'

She left the room and he sank into a chair and undid his cravat. Lizzie, the woman he loved, and Anne, the friend he would have loved. Together. In New York, where morality looked the other way. He imagined himself in summer whites on Fire Island, a high sun overhead, watching Lizzie and Anne wade into the ocean. He imagined his hands holding theirs, his embrace enfolding their tiny bodies simultaneously, his mouth moving over his wife's lips, his fingers caressing the inside of Anne's thigh. He would stride through the beach grass in that Atlantic cove looking for a place to make love in the sun.

'The sunflowers were my idea, actually,' Anne said. 'I told you, Mrs Whitley, they simply are the last word in all of the proper homes these days.'

'They are very lovely. Anne has such a gift for picking out the most charming flowers,' Sarah replied.

'Oh she always has,' Lizzie replied. 'When we were traveling on the continent together, she had the most remarkable ability to search out the most elegant flower markets. And in places you wouldn't look, either. Rouen, for example.'

'Rouen has a very colorful history,' Louis cut in. 'If you don't mind the smell of tanners' stalls in the middle of town.'

'They weren't all that bad,' Lizzie said. 'I think it rather depends on which way the wind blows.'

They all laughed at the table. Louis sat opposite of Anne and her eyes sparkled in the light of the lamps, in the crystal goblets that surrounded them, in the polished old silver the Whitleys used. The wine both suffused and aroused old sentiments within him. He remembered the breeze that had come through a field of yellowing wheat somewhere in the past, so satisfying, that he had fallen asleep on a flannel blanket under an immense elm. Had it all been a dream? He had kissed Anne that afternoon, when no one was looking... or it seemed as if no one was looking...

'I feel very much obligated to go to France again,' Anne said. 'One hears so much of the very serious developments with regards to art, particularly architecture.'

'I am reminded,' Louis said, putting his wine glass down, 'of that great monstrosity some madman named Eiffel is making on the Champs Elysées. A tower. Entirely of iron! Can you imagine such a thing? Surely there must be some limitations in the minds of powerful men than such a disgusting affront to the senses.'

'Oh I don't know, I think it'd look rather nice,' Anne said. 'I would expect such a thing to have a purpose. Rather like your apparatus. You're not just making the apparatus to sate the curiosity of some madcap investor, are you?'

'No, not *at all*,' Louis replied. 'The receiver will speak

for itself. My intention is to make it available for the use and benefit of all people. That's what photography is, a great equalizer. Daguerre told me so himself.'

'Forgive me, Louis,' Anne replied. 'I am not familiar with the moral aims of photography.'

Here Louis felt a sudden surge of self-righteous energy.

'The receiver is for artistic and social benefit, I assure you. And furthermore...'

'Better yet,' Anne replied, 'Let us assume that when you finish this endeavor, how will you prove to the world that it exists? Do you intend to show your work to the public?'

'Of course, it would be preposterous not to—'

'Perhaps it is better that we change the subject,' Lizzie said.

'Hear hear,' Sarah said. 'All this talk of progress makes me quite despondent. Where is Marie?'

'I believe she's having her dinner in the kitchen, Mamma,' Lizzie replied.

'It's best to leave her there,' Joseph replied. 'Are you

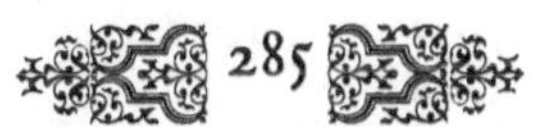

feeling ill, Mrs Whitley?'

'No, not particularly. Lizzie darling, remind me to have Marie turn down the beds a little early. I think I'll retire early this evening.'

'I'll come upstairs with you, Mamma.'

Louis and Anne stared at each other from across the table. Their exchange felt awkward, ill-placed. Between them sat Louis' son and Louis' father-in-law.

'I shouldn't have been so critical,' Louis said. 'I have upset her.'

'She's been keyed up all day,' Joseph replied. 'She was excited to see all of you, as was I. What do you say, my boy? Shall we finish our game of draughts in the parlor and leave your father to muse on iron towers and the great Daguerre? Care to join us, Miss Hartley?'

'Oh, no thank you, sir. I am so very tired.'

'Very well then,' Joseph said, rising from the table. 'Shall we, Adolphe?'

'You may retire at whatever hour you wish, young man,' Louis said to Adolphe. 'But no cigars and no brandy.'

Adolphe and Joseph left the table, leaving Anne and

Roundhay Garden Scene

Louis in the profound silence of the dinner table.

'Were the sunflowers really your idea?' he asked Anne.

'In a way,' she replied. 'There were sunflowers in your mother's house on the day that you first kissed me.'

He sank like a stone before the fire in the library. All around the house creaked: footsteps fell, doors closed, the clock ticked, the fire roared momentarily, died down, roared up again, popped out sparks, told its perfunctory tale. He heard voices:

'Goodnight, Mr Whitley.'

'Goodnight, my dear girl.'

A door gently clicked shut. Two or three more footsteps.

He could sense her hovering behind the library door, too afraid to enter. What if she did? What if, he imagined, she were naked, waiting for him to open it? She carried the scent of violet-leaf and rain with her; her scent was unmistakable. Even now it crept under the door, and he could smell it over the scent of the fire.

Another set of footsteps. She had walked away.

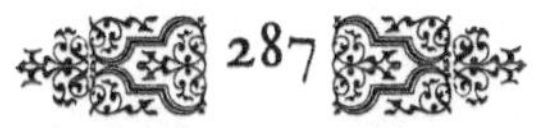

Sereno

He could hear another set of footsteps upstairs. Belle-mère retiring for the evening. Then Adolphe, his voice humming a tune, heading for the bathroom. Then Lizzie arrived in a nightgown, barefoot.

Her voice.

'But don't you worry about us,' Lizzie said, right as ten had struck. She had knocked gently on the door while Louis pretended to read. 'I'll sleep with her tonight. That cough has me worried.'

'You should look after her. I am also very concerned for her.'

'I suppose I'll see you tomorrow then, my dear.'

'Goodnight, *ma chère.*'

The door clicked closed. He stared into the fire again.

La femme de Monsieur Le Prince, as always, ensuring harmony in the house. He sank back in the worn green wingback chair. By now he'd pulled the cravat loose and undid a button to ventilate. He felt paralyzed. *Open the window, you fool,* he said to himself but even that was too daunting, too risky. The sweat formed under his armpits, the lust stirring itself under the woolen trousers he had on. Upstairs was his robe of Japanese silk, his slippers and pipe, but the chance of being alone with Anne while the house slept was overwhelming.

Minutes passed. Upstairs she was surely waiting for him. Lost in the jumble of his thoughts were memories of why they couldn't be together: it was there in a tumble of blue velvet, a broken glass, a poorly conceived apology or else something entirely trifling and useless, a sapphire night in 1868. Anne, iron-jawed and practically hermetic, unresolvable. *Ah, that's the reason I couldn't have her then, he thought. Because she couldn't be communicated with.*

And meanwhile the receiver looked on, mute and blameless, inured to the feeble limitations of human desire, impartial and unconcerned.

Anne was impermeable but present, able to hold a man to the coals but unable to resist the pull of years of unrequited desire. He wavered for a few moments before arising. It was late now; the mantle clock struck one. Only God and Death knew what he was about to do.

He undressed in the cold guest room where he and Lizzie slept. The moonlight flooded the floor with beautiful pale light. At the end of the hall was Sarah's room. He heard Lizzie reading to herself as she usually did—she had always been the kind of girl to stay up late and talk. He pulled a crisp and loose-fitting white nightshirt over himself. The cool cotton descended over his naked body and he felt alive and young again, enervated by his lust. He left the door to his room ajar and tiptoed to Lizzie's room. Gently he clasped the knob to Lizzie's room and opened it.

Indeed, she'd been reading to herself. She'd been in her own chair awaiting the inevitable to happen, in a white cotton nightgown of her own. She'd been waiting for him.

He sank to his knees on the carpet in front of her and buried his face in the soft earth of her body. He kissed the inside of her thighs, went deeper until he felt her opening her lap to him. She ran her fingers through the curls of his hair, in his whiskers, over his shoulders. Her body initially struggled to apprehend this communicable language that Louis spoke with his mouth and his hands. He pulled the nightgown off of her and she sat there, wide-legged and bare-breasted in the chair, moistened with sweat and warmed by the fire, her chest heaving while he kissed her in every secret place, in every fold of flesh, every dark bend and ripple of herself. His mouth moved from her crotch to her stomach, over her belly button; she moved his hands over her tiny breasts until his gigantic calloused palms covered them. She slid her body off of the chair and onto the floor, and lay spread-eagle before the fire. Louis pulled off his nightshirt. He looked deeply in her eyes before kissing her mouth, ringing her lips with his, commingling the scent of her cunt with the taste of his breath. She raised her legs until they were around his waist, until he was all the way deep down inside of her, and he felt the fulness of her being pulse and ripple and quiver all around him. He felt her press his fingers into the muscles of his back while he thrusted deep and hard, savoring the ocean salt of her flesh. Together they wrestled out the details of their lust.

She rolled him off of her and mounted him. His eyes filled with little gold stars as she descended on him, and the dazzling feeling shook him to distracted frenzy. In him he felt the surge and rush of the years falling fast behind him, until her face was all he could focus on, until the sound of his heavy breathing dulled in his ears and his fingers had reached into Anne's mouth to silence her climax. When she did it came as a soft cooing that escaped in a brief, mournful cry, and then... no more. Her breasts heaved, sighing away the lust, face upturned toward the ceiling. When she turned her gaze back toward him, he noticed the longing hadn't abated; instead, it had deepened. Here it was, every ponderous inch of their imperfect love expressed in solely physical terms, and still, after their first interlude in years, that ruinous feeling that they could not be together was not assuaged.

'I love you so much,' Louis said.

'You mustn't say things like that,' Anne whispered.

'She wants you to come with us.'

'Who? Lizzie?'

'Yes, Lizzie.'

'To where, Louis?'

'To America, Anne. And I want you to come, too. No one gave you a chance. I know you didn't want John. I know you wanted me.'

'I have my own life to lead, Louis.'

'But I want to live in it,' Louis said, gently. 'I want to see and love the things you love, too. I want to show you places you've always wanted to see. We could travel together. Paint still lives together.'

'Life does not work that way.' She rolled over him and lay on her side. His body felt immense next to hers. 'I made some very clear choices, Louis. You did, as well.'

She led him to the door. Kissed him gently on the cheek.

'Sleep well, my darling Louis,' she said.

Roundhay Garden Scene

She was right. Their lives had branched off into two different places, like the country roads that bounded over hillsides covered in Scotch broom. She had dingy, smoky Leeds and the Whitleys and maybe a few wealthy girls to teach watercolor to while Louis had the rest of the world and everything in it, including all the heartache and trouble it brought. He had the money but also the precarity, the cynical trust of businessmen and the boorish nouveau-riches swelled to surfeit on a diet of scorn and scandal. She wanted no part of that world, he realized as he lay in bed, waiting for the sun to rise and the noisy world to burst in. What she had wanted was solitude, and she had attained solitude by refusing the thing that had only given her pleasure. What need would she have had of the world? What could have Louis provided, married and secure, cajoling his American investors with the receiver? And when he realized that her hermeticism was self-imposed, he felt immensely sorry for her. He lamented that he could not have loved her more.

But could it be that one day Lizzie might die. Isn't that what happened all the time? Didn't people die, young people, old people? Wouldn't it be easier for Lizzie to die and then Anne to become the convenient second wife? Or, maybe under that same oak tree in Sodom, why not both? To have wife and mistress, clad in white, bare-breasted, smelling of apples, tasting of sin? Why not that life instead? It was permissible—if you had enough money to forget about other people.

Deep down, he wanted to revisit the moment he first touched her. Where was it again? Provence? Normandy? A farm in the Somme? The Lake Country? If only the receiver had been there... they'd gone punting on the river... a nameless, faceless river, blue as a dream, rolled by without a murmur. Flies hovered over the surface, an angler with a bad eye stood barefoot in the warm water nearby...there were crickets. She'd been wearing a white dress, they'd been picnicking on a white flannel blanket... she'd left her bonnet out...it flew away in the warm breeze that came in the afternoon. They'd been eating ripe cherries and the juice stained her fingers, and she kissed away the scarlet drops gently, discreetly, while he guided her hand down to his trousers...she had touched him there for a searing instant, sweat beading on his forehead and he had whispered, *ma chère mademoiselle, mon bébé*, all the French delicacies he'd learn to coo into the ears of English and German whores. And that evening Lizzie came to him, like a goddess of twilight, her black satin shawl billowing in an arc, and she let him smell the one or two drops of rose perfume she'd let fall like amber tears onto the soft white down of her breasts. Isis in a mist of fireflies.

He whispered to the shadowy figure hiding behind

the privet, just as the morning drizzle finished depositing its largesse of silver drops on the last of the white roses: 'I don't know why you're hiding, but you don't have to.'

'I am ashamed, Louis.'

'Ashamed? Ashamed of what?'

She moved aside a wet branch of privet and emerged into the sunlight. Drops of water beaded on her grey-green velvet jacket.

'I don't want to look at Lizzie.'

'Lizzie doesn't know. She doesn't have to.'

'I should go home; I don't feel well...'

He took her arm as she passed him and curved her into his embrace. She did not relent—she still felt desire for him. The feeling was mutual. He had awoken desiring Lizzie and Anne in bed with him, with only the receiver to record his lust, his love for these two beautiful women.

'Stay,' he said, looking into her eyes. 'I want you to stay with me.'

'I couldn't...' she replied.

He kissed her and she wrapped an arm around his

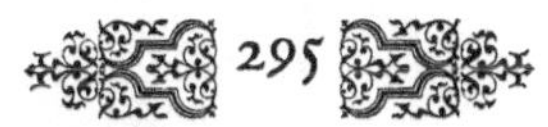

neck.

This was dangerous, mortally dangerous. Any moment Lizzie could step out, or Sarah. Her ears hearkened to the sound of the carriage wheels on the gravel outside, the familiar slam of the carriage-house gate, Joseph's cough in the cool October air.

'I want you to stay. Let me photograph you, Anne. Let me touch you before I let you go back to your mother's house.'

'This evening?'

He nodded. 'When all this is done. I shall come and visit you in your room again. Come to America with me. I beg you to consider.'

'I can't, Louis,' she said, breaking away. 'What you are asking me to do is uproot everything I know, everything I love, to accompany you and your wife. You want me as a mistress. Say that you do.'

'I do not want you as a mistress, Anne.'

Her eyes filled with tears. 'Then what else can I be?'

'My friend, my lover...'

'Where, Louis? In New York? Does society not exist

in New York? Do people of good morals not exist there? Where will you keep me if I go? Where am I to find work, if I am to be your mistress? Do you expect me to model for sculptors like the other women you've sinned with?'

'I don't know,' Louis replied. 'But I am asking you to at least accompany us.'

'Why feel sorry for me? I am perfectly content here,' she said. 'Ah. Now I see. This is Lizzie's idea. You both feel sorry for me, because of what happened with John.'

Louis shook his head and put his hands on his hips. The sun emerged from behind a cloud and filled the terrace with warm afternoon light. Anne now trembled, her chest heaving, her breathing short.

'I really must be leaving now, I'm sorry.'

She started to go into the house. He took her arm again. This time, she did not look back.

'Then at least stay for supper. This afternoon I will photograph with the receiver.'

She turned around and gave Louis a fierce look. In her eyes—in that light—was the dark of the Thames, limpid and murky. A tear had fallen from her eyes and he caught it with his index finger. She was leaving because she loved him, couldn't bare to be relegated to the niche he'd made for her, he realized. He'd stared into those eyes on fragrant nights where the sound of the waltz was muffled by his desire for Anne, for Lizzie, bending over to stare into the starlight reflected in the waters of a fountain. She didn't want John because she didn't know whom she wanted. Louis had always been the easy choice.

He followed her into the library. She feigned gathering up a blueprint for the receiver, and he traced the inky lines of the schematics with his fingertip, traced a cross into them over and over again. She rested her head against his shoulder and closed her eyes. He could smell the faint scent of milled soap, the smell of violets on her, the rain, the mist that settled over the Yorkshire meadows. Silent and unassuming, she guided his hands up down over the soft fabric of her bodice. He wrapped his arms around her—his big strong arms—arms that rowed boats and molded kaolin clay. She felt like a bony little bird fearfully but vividly shaking from the cold. He felt his whiskers bristle against her neck, followed by his strong wet kisses. He pushed up her against the library wall. The master of the mysterious receiver now dared to press his erect self into her, to make grotesque love to her there among the wicked philosophers of the past. She pushed down his jacket, undid his cravat and unbuttoned his shirt and trousers. He pressed his mouth against her, suffocated her with his lust; her hands moved down until they held the fiery bolt thrusting up against all of her imagined lines. She pushed his trousers down until they were around his ankles, until she could feel the bracing heat of his hairy legs entwined in the grey-green taffeta of her day dress. Until he could feel the course hair of his legs on hers.

'I love you,' he said, over and over again. 'You are the source of my art. I never have ever stopped loving you. I never will.'

She said nothing, but her heart raced, fluttered at the sound of his voice in her ears and the feel of his foreskin in her hands, moist and dewy like the skin under her corset.

His eyes centered on the places he wanted to explore: her mouth, her eyes, her breasts, the calm silent space where he'd fingered her before. In this rarified field, he saw two figures emerging from a single point in a deep blue field of stars. It was Lizzie and Anne, cosmic and radiant, merging into a singular, voluptuous figure made of warm honeyed skin, bathed in silky windblown coral-colored cloth. Venus Anadyomene—just like the Poussin he'd seen once long ago in a hall in the Louvre—but it would be he, instead of grey-bearded old Neptune, who would enjoy the splendor of this callipygian Aphrodite made of starlight coming to him on an immense clamshell. The receiver's lens emerged behind her like an aureole, enveloping her, framing her, this starry virgin with her ancient crotales, an assimilated Lizzie and Anne with four arms, four legs, two gorgeous breasts the color of moonlight, with eyes of mother-of-pearl and sapphires dangling from coral bracelets.

'I can't keep up much longer,' he said, panting, shaking with all the energy he could muster. Anne watched his expression move from blissful bewilderment to release. He bent his knees and uttered a loud, impassioned shout. Anne watched the fat milky drops spill on the parquet tiles of the library floor.

He opened his eyes and saw Anne staring innocently at him. She was unrecognizable, a woman he had seen on the street once, Parisian and anonymous. Suddenly he knew why she had felt the way she did. Their tryst was indeed shameful. For an instant, he saw Lizzie in Anne's place, bewildered and unsure. His breath stilled and his heart stopped thundering. He saw the beast that Anne had seen and tried to fend off, and it was hideous.

He heard footsteps on the gravel. A door opening. Adolphe's quick footsteps, then Lizzie and Sarah's chatter, the sound of Sarah's cane striking the floor. The Lord arriving in the cool of the afternoon. Anne whisked herself out of the room and closed the library door behind her.

'Are you feeling better?' he heard Lizzie say.

'Oh yes, much better,' Anne replied. 'I had the most terrible headache this morning. Mrs Whitley: How was church?'

'It was most agreeable, a very proper sermon, I believe.

Roundhay Garden Scene

Mr Whitley does not seem to agree with me, though.'

'He spoke too much,' Joseph said. 'The vicar is too literary, far too mystical for me. It was all very forgettable.'

Louis pulled up his trousers and tucked in his shirt, pulled up his suspenders. She was creating a distraction for him, allowing him a quick escape, if he wanted. He took out a handkerchief and sopped up the mess on the ground, and stuffed it in his back pocket.

'Where is Louis?'

'I was just wondering myself,' Anne replied. 'I came down to get a spot of tea but he's nowhere to be found.'

The library door opened and Lizzie appeared.

'Monsieur Le Prince, we've been looking all over for you. Are you busy?'

'I'm always busy,' he replied, breathlessly. *Ma femme.* How was church?'

The film. The camera. The light. The perfect weather. The big beautiful branches. The sunlight. A breeze that lifted the branches, scattered the leaves, made ripples in the surface of the river. The scattered light that broke through the branches. Dew dashed from fronds spattered on the terrace. The film. At last, in place. The camera lens, a perfect black eye under the shade of the ivy that devoured the brick wall. The light. The camera. The film.

The light had slanted into an angle, diaphanous and exquisite, that rendered the terrace before the library brilliant, golden and unwaveringly proportional. One by one they all filed out of the house, these would-be actors, into the afternoon sun. Joseph and Sarah were still attired in the clothing they'd worn to church—Sarah's tippet giving her a touch of the odd and exotic, an old bird-of-paradise hobbling on one foot, Joseph wearing the long grey woolen coat some furrier had given him in Boston long ago. Adolphe had changed into his favorite coat and the trousers that were too short for his tall frame. And Anne, of course—his favorite—the solitary and taciturn Anne, her grey-green dress, her odd little hat, the black bustle on her backside, strange and silent.

'You mean to photograph *us*, darling?' Lizzie said.

'Of course,' Louis said. 'The whole purpose is to determine the motion of the hand crank and whether the impressions can be properly made with the lens at the current calibration.'

'I hope this will not take all afternoon,' Sarah said. 'The weather is nice, but one does not know when it might change.'

Roundhay Garden Scene

'I agree with Mrs Whitley,' Joseph said. 'And besides, Louis, I am afraid you may not have enough daylight.'

'I disagree,' Louis said. 'Adolphe, *mon fils*, start walking in circles around Miss Hartley.'

Adolphe began at a brisk walking pace. He circled Anne, once, twice, three times, four times in a circle around them, picking up speed with every turn. Anne held a hand against her brow.

'And what do you want *me* to do, Louis?'

'Walk backward in a circle,' Lizzie replied, from behind him. 'Don't be so shy, Anne, you look very fine today.'

Instinctively, Mr and Mrs Whitley began to walk together in a circle around Adolphe. The breeze picked up. A few leaves scattered on the terrace gravel.

'Continue until I say you are to move no more!' Louis said.

He removed the cloth from the receiver. Light flooded the viewfinder and he saw this human orrery rendered upside down and backward in a soft haze of muted colors.

He turned the hand-crank gently. The paper film stirred from its cassette; quickly it received just an instant of light, a flicker of perfect autumn light with all its motes of dust and notes of gold floated infinitesimally into the lacquered abyss where the darkness consigned the image. Louis turned the crank and at 12 frames a second the family danced in a circle, was sketched out in silver on the gelatin. In-between Adolphe's skipping around and the Whitleys hobbling away, his eyes centered on the shape of Anne's body, how its form caught the sunlight and how her dress pleats made shadows—and she intuitively turned her back on him, away from view.

The film spooled into the other cassette. There was no more paper left on which to film.

'Stop now,' he said.

He looked up from the receiver. The world continued onward, silently, assured of its power and its security. No one else had dared to steal from Almighty God two seconds of His time—painters had in the past, perhaps a few poets, but no one who had harnessed light itself and mutely transformed its contours to fit neatly into the square of silver gelatin. Everything that that solitary and sublime October afternoon had ever been—everything that had created it, life itself—now sat silently transfixed for all time, if possible, on a single strip of paper.

'The experiment was a success, unequivocally so,' Louis said, caressing Anne's hand. They'd absconded to the library as the rain was beginning to fall on the roof. 'Thank you, ma chère. Thank you for being part of this.'

'There'll be more,' Anne said. 'You'll make more, I'm sure. It'll be wonderful for you and your family.'

'In Paris, next year, I hope. Here, let me show you something.'

He took her hand and led her to the portfolio. He pulled out a new sheet of paper on which he had sketched out another great mysterious box, full of cranks and wheels and glass eyes.

'The deliverer. I can start building it when I return from America, once I have secured investors for it. Next year—when the lilacs are in bloom—you and I will go to the Exposition and we shall see how the public reacts to this. It will be named for you, *chérie.*'

Anne imagined what it would be like walking with Louis in Paris during lilac time. She imagined the steel-grey morning suit he'd wear, the leather of his shoes, the smell of lilacs in the Champs Elysées that she had only heard of. His champagne-flavored kisses, the soft crush of red velvet of a theatre box, with Lizzie in a haze of twilight-colored tulle, and of course, her paintings on display next to his and a thousand other artists at one of those vaunted salons in the home of a rich nobody. She luxuriated in the firelight-glow of Louis' features, so inviting and gentle. He could be a great lover beyond all that lust and madness. It was easy to see why Lizzie had learned to love him despite all that he had done.

'That was a lovely dinner, wasn't it?'

'It was,' Anne said. 'It's nice that we sent Marie home for the evening. Does she usually get Sundays off to see her mother?'

'No,' Louis replied. 'As far as I know, she rarely gets to see her.'

'The poor girl!' Anne replied.

'It means I can visit you in the dark again…without having to wake her up. Once more, before I leave for home tomorrow,' Louis whispered.

He leaned into kiss her gently. She was a little reluctant but her body felt again the pulse of longing for him, especially in the high surge of his achievement. Their lips touched and she felt faint from the roaring fire in the library and his indomitable presence.

The library door opened.

'Anne darling, would you care to help me to bed? I've…'

Sarah's cane had barely crossed the threshold. She had turned her glance to the windows, and then to the fireplace, expecting to find Anne reading in the chair she had always sat in when she visited the Whitleys.

Anne pushed Louis off of her. Louis' eyes darted towards Sarah and then toward Anne, and then back to Sarah.

'*Belle-mère*—I was—'

Louis watched as Sarah's face turned pale with shock. She tripped over the threshold and fell backward against the wall. Her cane knocked over the whatnot and a china vase of lilies crashed to the floor.

Lizzie rushed down the stairs.

'What's happened?' she said.

'Fetch some water, Lizzie,' Anne said, a great regret coming over her. 'I'm coming, Mrs Whitley, I'm *coming*.'

Sarah had seen too much, walked too much, breathed too much stale night air. This was just another drachm of poison, another overexertion of nervous activity, this coughing. Clapped in bed with a hot water bottle, Sarah managed to roll out for Lizzie what she had seen in frank terms. No, it didn't happen that way, Lizzie said, cooing her mother's rabid anxiety, teasing the horror so it would lay flat in bed with her. She took her hand and stroked out the wrinkles again and again. It was just an illusion. Louis hovered behind Sarah's bedroom door, listening to them talk. An illusion? Of course. An illusion. A dream. Something not seen, only imagined. What sly trickeries artists could sketch out on paper they could construct in libraries, rendezvouses and midnight visits. Lizzie soothed her voice, threw a blanket over her mother.

'Mamma, you mustn't speak now. You had an attack, that is all.'

A bitter, wet cough responded to it, as if to defy Lizzie.

Louis ran a nervous hand through his hair. If she recovered? Insisted upon it? How then would dinner go? She'd never look at him the same way.

And then, shutting his eyes, he thought of Anne, of escaping to Paris with her, kissing her under a gazebo surrounded by almond blossoms.

It could happen... all he had to pack his bag... escape, break a door, a window, run out into the evening rain with her.

'No, no,' Sarah weakly replied. 'I saw them both.'

He waited for her coughing to subside. Lizzie stepped out and took her husband into the parlor.

'She's adamant that she saw you and Anne. In some... indiscretion. I don't believe her, Louis. But I do think you should tell me what did happen.'

Poor, miserable, burdened Lizzie, faultless and clueless. He looked down on her and in all his guilt understood that she knew he had kissed another woman. How could he not to? These things had to be parsed in a way that couldn't ruin everything. She knew about certain visits to certain boulevards in certain faubourgs in Paris, certain photographic materials passed under butcher paper envelopes or stuck in the pages of expensive books borrowed from friends.

'I was... merely consoling Anne. She was... afraid of coming to New York with us. I wanted to merely make our sentiments known to her.'

'This weekend has been very trying for Mamma,' Lizzie replied. She rolled a cigarette from the tray on the mantle. She lit it with a long piece of straw from the fireplace, exhaled the smoke slowly. 'You must realize, Louis. If she is ill it is because she has taxed herself so. All this she did for us and for Miss Hartley. And look at her now. My poor mother.'

Louis sat emotionless opposite her, watching the very manly habit she'd picked up from him.

'The things we've done, Louis. Your receiver. Our travels to America.' She flicked the ashes into the fire. 'We're to blame, dear. It's us. Whatever we've done, now or in the past. Whatever it might be, darling.'

'I know,' Louis said, with no emotion in his voice. 'I don't wish to give her anymore grief, my love. I can give Miss Anne a ride home.'

'We'd better let Father do that,' Lizzie replied sharply. 'We don't want any more rude shocks.'

They could hear Sarah coughing loudly again, as Marie changed the hot water bottle once more. There was a tinkling of china, an administering of medicine, a few spoken words, footsteps, then peace again.

Louis came in and sat in the chair next to Sarah. When she was not coughing she was wheezing, mouth half-open and eyes glazed over. When her eyes caught him she turned her head and closed them.

He heard Lizzie and Anne talking at the base of the stairs, without raising their voices. Not a word of goodbye. He was sure she was kicking her out of the house, revoking her access to Louis. He remembered the introduction his mother had given him to her lady friends once: *here is my son Louis, a singular kind of boy that can make a grown woman cry.* The weight of this guilt was now making it extremely difficult to breathe.

Marie Lizzie ducked back in to check on Sarah.

'I'll sleep here tonight with you, Mamma. I'll have Marie fetch the doctor.'

'You are too kind,' Sarah said, her voice barely rising above the haze of her wheezing. Lizzie took her mother's hand and sat on the bed, stroked a few grey hairs from her face. Sarah stared back at Louis, nodding off on the couch. Louis tried to fixate his gaze on her bleary, heartbroken eyes, as if to relay an apology telepathically to her, but sleep came faster than his thoughts could. He rested his head against the wing of a chair, and folded his hands as if to show her he was praying. When he awoke an hour later Lizzie had thrown a blanket on him and was sitting quietly watching Sarah sleep.

'I was thinking,' Lizzie said, quietly, not turning toward him. 'I believe it's best to go to America, just you and me and Adolphe. Better to spare anyone else any more heartache, don't you think?'

'I'll fetch us some tea,' Louis replied.

The doctor came at midnight.

He held his ear to her tiny frame and heard her inhale. Exhale. Inhale. The doctor raised a hand and everyone stopped breathing. Marie held her breath, and Louis restrained the air in his nostrils. In that air, he figured, the disease ravaging Sarah's lungs could hang pregnant, waiting to descend into someone else's shocked little body.

'Infectious pneumonia,' the doctor grimly pronounced. He looked at Marie as he pocketed his watch into his lapel. 'Boil the linens. Put a pan of coals under the bed.'

'Pneumonia?' Lizzie said, gasping for air as if she had been gutted alive.

'The evening air is malodorous and dangerous to her health. If I've seen it once, I've seen it a thousand times. I warned her not to venture out into the autumn air. We know not what it may contain.'

Louis heard his own admonition ring out in his temples like a tocsin: *You must be very careful of the night air, my dear Mrs Whitley...*

But of course, the evening air, in this part of the world at least, was full of contagion and misfortune. And he thought to himself, it had been his fault for dragging her out of confinement to play with his little contraption in a garden full of dew drops, mud puddles, and shade. Louis felt heaved with guilt. Wasn't it just like her to do too much for the people she loved? Wouldn't that always be her fault, caring too much?

Sarah stirred a little.

'Doctor Forsyth,' she said. 'Marie, fetch a glass of cordial for the man—'

'We haven't any, ma'am. Just rest still,' Marie replied.

'Not for ten years. Not since John lived here,' Joseph said.

Lizzie rose from bed and wrapped the shawl tightly around her shoulders.

'Monsieur Le Prince, come attend to me.'

Louis looked at his poor helpless wife, a woman thrust into responsibilities that were not hers to assume. Sarah was on her deathbed. Arrayed all around her were helpless grey and brown figures who mutely assumed their places in her life, maid and doctor and father. And Lizzie now was in Sarah's place, or would be soon, anyway. Joseph, who really had no capacity for vivid emotions, shook his head in defeat at the foot of his wife's bed. As if her sickness were a mere inconvenience, a spell of rain on a half-decent summer afternoon. She'd never rise from this place, never settle in a grand gesture of world-weary fatigue in her great chair in the parlor, a glass of sherry in one hand and a dish of Swiss bonbons from a tin in the other, to make a casual observation on the weather. Never again.

Sereno

It rained again. The rain, as always in this part of England, came on gently, the sound of its patter starting in the elms where the road petered out at the gate to the house. Louis could hear it advance, almost as if it were a line of infantrymen. Finally—when the arc of the storm cloud had reached the apex of the roof—it remained there and advanced no further. All night it rained, rained and rained, and in the morning a brief but loud shower of hail accompanied Marie and Lizzie up the stairs to check on Sarah. Louis saw the rain in the dark of his tired eyelids, and felt the patter on his shoulders, even though he was indoors.

The last thing Sarah asked for was a letter from Anne. When no letter could be produced, Lizzie wrote to Anne, and Anne sent back a tender little letter addressed to Sarah. Lizzie sat on her bed and read it to Sarah twice.

'Anne is such a terribly sentimental young lady,' Sarah said.

Lizzie wiped two great tears from her eyes and squeezed her mother's hands. 'Yes, Mamma, that is true...'

'She would have made a very great match for John, or for Louis.'

'Ah, is that so? You really think that?'

Sarah swallowed and blinked slowly. She nodded her head gently.

Lizzie wept again. To go from dream to nightmare in just four days. To go from sun and warm air to grey skies and rain, to pneumonia weather and pneumonia itself; to lose everything after having gained every signal comfort of family togetherness. A tragedy.

'I have a gift for you, from Marie, *belle-mère*,' Louis said.

'How much is it?' Sarah said, in a delirious haze.

'It's free; it's your favorite blanket,' Louis replied.

'Quick, get me my purse,' Sarah said, gesturing blindly to Marie.

Instead Louis threw the blanket over Sarah and tucked it in under her tiny body.

Marie had drawn the curtains and lit a few tapers. The house may have just as well become unmoored, Louis figured, and drifted in the torrent out to sea. Lizzie could feel death approach from outside. It came in on little cat's feet with the rain, pooled itself in a cold little puddle at the threshold. Then it tracked itself in with the visitors: the vicar, the friends, the relatives all coming to say goodbye.

Louis watched them all come in, handkerchiefs pressed to mouths, people in threes or in fives, people he'd never known in all of his years of married life. Most of them were neighbors, people who'd known the Whitleys in business or through church. And with each group, Lizzie would gesture gently toward Louis, standing at the sill, watching the rain make great puddles in the yard: *this is my husband, Monsieur Le Prince.* Of course everyone knew who he was. The Frenchman in Roundhay, the Paris émigré, adopted son of the great Daguerre. Rumor was that he had met some of the Pre-Raphaelites in Cambridge one summer in the sixties and had perhaps attended a soirée which he vaguely remembered. These nameless visitors, all muttonchops and lace dickies and fear, all looked on him apprehensively.

When death was perceived close enough to the door, Lizzie opened it and let death walk in. She filled Sarah's room with chairs. She had Marie fill vases with water and sent for flowers. The flowers arrived from the market, rain-kissed and in great folds of brown paper. Big white and yellow chrysanthemums. Marie invited her cousin to come and cook for the family so that she could help Sarah to die, and this cousin sent up, almost every four hours, the same blancmange of sweetened rice that reminded Louis of the kind his late grandmother once made. Then the vicar came with surplice and stole and commended her soul to God. Sarah swallowed, blinked, and then gently closed her eyes, her mind immured by the pneumonia now drowning her alive and disgusted by the spectators watching her die. Sarah's room stank of white flowers, incense and camphor; it was a miracle, Louis thought, that no one else had bothered to get sick.

She died slowly. Deliberately. The weather worsened; the rain did not abate. Louis imagined it was falling inside the house now, inundating the room where John used to live and cascading liberally down the staircase.

And then came Wednesday, 24 October. On that day the rains broke in the afternoon and the blue sky appeared, punctuated with great puffy white clouds. The room brightened. A faint blue hue appeared in the folds of Sarah's white linen blankets, light from a window whose curtains Marie parted. Louis got up to look out on the garden. Anne hadn't come—and everyone knew why—despite being an obvious family friend. She had written back earlier in the day, feigning some polite excuse, a socially acceptable negation, with a boilerplate apology. He looked back and saw Lizzie kneeling on the floor before her mother, sobbing into the blankets. He reproached himself for wanting to see Anne when Lizzie was suffering so much.

Louis tapped the window with his finger.

The birds ceased their chirping and scattered out of the trees and flew away into the sky.

Louis sat back down at Sarah's bedside. He looked at

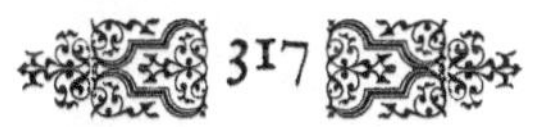

317

Sereno

Sarah.

'*Belle-mère*,' he heard himself say. 'Madame Sarah.'

He grasped her hand. It was limp, cold.

Her eyes were still open, her gaze fixed on the window outside.

She died watching him watch the sparrows. It was then that Louis forgot about Anne Hartley, or the receiver, or the deliverer, or Paris, or the paper negatives, or Mr Eastman, or America.

In the haze of his grief, Louis eventually developed the frames from the fateful October day that had taken his mother-in-law to her grave. In the darkroom at the brass foundry, he saw her image bloom and reemerge from the warm toxic sea of the emulsified past. There she was, at seven frames a second. Her tippet, her face, her awkward gait. Her cane. The way she leant on it. Even in the darkroom, he yearned for the predictability of her presence, its lassitude, the chagrin of her old body. When they brought her out for burial he marveled at how tiny she was, how little and frail she was under those petticoats and garnitures and chemises, how closely the black fabric swaddled her face, borne to eternity in her coffin, in a calming ruffle of black Alençon lace and crêpe.

Roundhay Garden Scene

The grief and guilt weighted everything Louis did. When he was alone, he often thought of Anne. Of Anne's face. Of how her cunt tasted. How her breasts felt in his hands. How age had spared her face from its usual detractions. How even in middle age, he felt young with her, how liberated from the usual concerns of business and family life he was whenever she had even exhaled her sweet breath. He tried to muster up the courage to write to her, but he could never come to it. Instead, he took the receiver out around town, took a few pictures. He filmed Adolphe playing his accordion on the steps of Roundhay Cottage one grey afternoon. Another brilliant afternoon came and he recorded traffic over the Leeds bridge, the carriages rattling over the muddy cobblestones, steam still rising from the manure piles in the street.

With proof of the receiver's power now in tangible form, Louis wrote to his American investors. Planned a showing in New York. Rented a mansion in the same city in which to show these new... what were they called? Moving pictures? Cinematographs? Photokinesthethic displays, perhaps? Lizzie would have sent off to Selfridge's for dresses, but Louis told her to wait. There was a Universal Exposition in Paris to see. In Paris, she'd be fitted at Maison Worth— nothing extravagant, of course, but something fitting for an eventual outing among the smart set on Park Avenue.

In Paris, they saw Monsieur Eiffel's steel monstrosity towering above the horse-chestnut trees on the Boulevard Haussmann, the June sun bestowing upon it a surreal and menacing character. Its presence was inescapable, its sinusoidal form reaching into the sky above as if to defy God. Louis wrote to his American investors, sent facsimiles, received invitations to salons, soirées, even a séance or two. The sting of Sarah's death had scarcely begun to heal when the creditors came calling, first at Roundhay and then at Louis' own house, and then in Paris, screaming at him from politely-penned letters. Everyone was living out of trunks: in Paris, in America, in Leeds, in London, in Calais where John now lived and worked. Thomas Edison arrived from America with a recording he'd made of the largest choir in living memory—some 4,000 people, the papers said—all singing a chorus from Handel's *Israel in Egypt*. Gentlemen crowded the palm-decked Hall of Music to listen to the ghostly voices on the wax cylinder intoning the power of the divine. Louis visited the ethnographic exhibits and longed to take a trip to Zanzibar to photograph a caravanserai. There were heliographs and kinetic and piezoelectric displays, magic lantern shows, hot press typesetters, clouds of Moroccan incense, crescendoes and swells of spirit organs and tabernacular harmoniums carved in ebony and surmounted by gilt angels, sprays of elegant and exotic flowers, suppers of turbot and sturgeon roe and *vol-au-vent à la financière*, flâcons of perfume and great pitchers of sparkling Burgundy and goblets of Malmsey wine, nights spent wandering energetically on the Champs-Elysées to attend some magnificent and debauched soirée in which the dinner was served à la réveillon as in the days of the wicked past, and in which husband and wife yearned for the blue arc of dawn to swing upwards over the zenith and propel them to sleep. And Louis dreamed, among the damask roses and fronds of ever-blooming lilacs and haunting aftertaste of absinthe, of the receiver and deliverer taking in the vast throngs of humanity ambling in the Hall of Machines, or to witness the surreal humming of a vast electric machine that would be both kaleidoscope and mirror of the world. He left calling-cards, invitations to tea, and was met with perfunctory, wavering interest. He bought Morris chairs, Persian rugs, bronze lamps, wall hangings, globe sconces, linen tablecloths. Lizzie at last received her dresses from Worth. They even managed to meet Singer Sargent just as he was heading off to Spain to paint some old grandee. When they returned from Paris, a solicitor in Leeds handed him a sheaf of papers, advising him that he was about to be sued by dozens of people.

Of course, the news had escaped certain cherried lips in Paris regarding Le Prince and his receiver. Naturally Edison had been there at some point, and his friends had made a special point to dine with Louis and Lizzie, and to ask about the receiver. Louis had already figured out by this time that, from a practical point of view, it was easier to use celluloid instead of paper film. Finding the celluloid would be easy; there were chemists ready to make it at half the cost it took to make in America. That was the easy part. Harder still was the search for another investor to supply the celluloid film. Perhaps there was a European investor. But looking for one took time and money, neither of which he had anymore. He instead looked forward to the day when he would abscond with Lizzie and Adolphe to New York City, not as tourists or as poor artists, but as American citizens, and in that rented mansion unveil to the public the beautiful and quietly wondrous machine to his new compatriots.

Then the year 1890 arrived. There was an exuberance in the air. Everyone had taken up eurhythmics and bicycling. The end of the nineteenth century was at hand. Louis' whiskers grew grayer; he was assuming the figure of an overworked, albeit somewhat still respectable, old man. He had managed to forget about Anne in the frenzy of 1889, and had assumed she had retained her place in the shadows of his memory. Maybe she had. There were occasional upwellings of regret and shame amid certain grey evenings in the winter, when the doldrums of the cold and the dark hollowed out his soul. Not even holding his wife close to him had inspired him like it used to. Every day in the mail, a chorus of disjointed and fragmented threats hounded him. The house was filled with an uneasy energy, as if it was all made of glass and at any minute a horde of creditors and lawyers and bailiffs might crash in. No solicitor of insurance within fifty miles would sell a policy to him. Instead, he wrote useless letters to the American and British patent offices with a request for an update. No one bothered to reply. The creditors came to seize Joseph's furniture as collateral, and the old man—

now confined to a wheelchair and in very poor health—looked on helplessly as his fine things were all taken away to sell at auction. Dinners at Roundhay were tense, febrile affairs. Sometimes there were scenes, words said, oaths taken.

In the midst of all of this, Albert, Louis' brother, wrote from Dijon inviting him to stay for a month or so, to get away from the bad weather in the north and to settle their mother's estate.

My darling Elizabeth, if some accident should befall me, know, my dearest, that my thoughts rest with you...

They could be fixed on no other woman...

No other woman...

My darling Elizabeth... ma femme, ma chérie...

Should some accident fall between us—between me in Paris and you there in Leeds—know that I love you and you alone.

You alone...

My darling Elizabeth. My beautiful wife.

Having finished a letter at his bureau, Louis rose,

arranged his briefcase, and stuffed a suitcase with clothing. He kissed his wife goodbye, gently, on the mouth, in the stuffy bedroom on a warm July day. He brushed the hairs away from her face and gazed into her blue eyes, ran a rough hand gently over the sweet soft flesh of her naked neck, on which the scent of white roses had faintly remained. Louis promised her he'd be back and they'd set sail for America immediately after his return. There was nothing to worry about, just a trip to see some cousins, sort out Mamma's inheritance. Louis kissed his son goodbye on the forehead, told him to behave, gave him a few pounds just in case. Louis left England for good in the middle of the night. *Pour prendre congé*: away on business, he told everyone. A few weeks to look after affairs, write a few letters to the Americans, send a few telegrams. Already the weight of his anxiety was making him gaunt and ill-kempt, and the crush of the years could be intimated, at least to valets and porters, behind certain railroad car veneers, beyond the wide views of the English countryside. In London, he thought he forgot his bill-fold on the train and spent a frantic hour looking in vain for it at the central office, only to find it in the right front pocket of his macintosh. It would be apropos to introduce himself now, he thought, as Louis Le Prince: visionary of the camera-eye, debtor, sinner, madman. *At your service.*

Onward to see John in Calais. On the steamer to Calais, he read a book of English history and wondered what falling through the ice-cold Atlantic might feel, how the pull of the water would drag him down into the deep and into a graveyard of medieval shipwrecks. How many thousands had made the same journey towards recognizable success only to have the sea open its mouth to swallow them whole. John looked older, heavier; the years had not been kind to him and the absence from close family had taken its toll. John served him tea in a whitewashed house on a spit of Norman land reaching into the Atlantic. They took their shoes off and strolled on the sand barefoot together, making plans, scoffing at fate, reveling in their own hubris.

At dinner in Calais one grey evening Louis said, 'I want you to understand something. Something that I should like you to tell my wife, if either one of you should ever meet again.'

'What is that, sir?' John said.

'That if anything should happen to me, it is imperative that the receiver be granted an American patent. I am afraid Edison is out to kill me. He has sent Pinkerton men after me.'

'You look as if you think me mad,' Louis finished, sensing John's shock by the way he had spit up his wine. 'I am not lying. The letters the lawyers have sent me have threatened my life, John. They are looking for blood or money. That is why I am leaving to Dijon. To escape.'

'Is that how bad things are, then? And Lizzie?'

'She is well provided-for, I assure you,' Louis replied.

Outside an errant sea swell hammered the yellow cliffs and its sound thundered in the half-darkened dining room like the sound of a distant gun.

In Dijon there were crickets. There were chickens. There were pink roses. There was long-lived twilight. There were young children—Albert Le Prince's, his brother's children—scurrying up the stairs, asking who he was. He heard the carts rattle over the cobblestones with an unusual delicacy, an ease that he had not heard in many years. Louis bought a straw hat and had a tiny glass of kir in a garden full of hollyhocks. Modernity and all of its excesses, relievedly, had not yet reached Dijon like it had in the capitals. Albert's wife still lit her hurricanes with oil, still referred to Albert as *mon épouse*, and pressed the same pink roses from her grandmother's garden close to her breast as if to distill, by osmosis almost, their fragrance into her skin.

He longed for Lizzie. Their lives could have been this easy: a house in Dijon, barefoot children, gushing fountains, a white wall, sunflowers. Maybe the receiver had become the Moloch to which Louis had sacrificed everything that mattered. Now the sacrifice was apparent.

He cried for his mother at her grave. To forget about it all, he escaped every night for an hour or two with Albert to visit a brothel in town, or to drink a glass of wine under the yellow lamps of a café *au plein air*. They talked of art incessantly. In Dijon there was art and oblivion and there were sunsets. In Dijon the linen bedsheets floated down majestically amid a cascade of golden motes caught in the sun as he watched their young maid make his bed.

The train had arrived fifteen minutes early.

He had packed light.

The station platform, naked and empty except for the dust that veiled the white bricks and the windows of the ticketing office. A bench. There, under a lamppost, the night watchman smoking his pipe and watching the planet Venus alight over the western hills from which the train would inexorably come.

Louis had said his goodbyes, made his intentions known.

'But when will we see Monsieur again, and Madame, and Monsieur's children?' asked Albert Le Prince's wife.

Louis knew better not to respond.

'Let the man be, Madame Le Prince,' Albert replied.

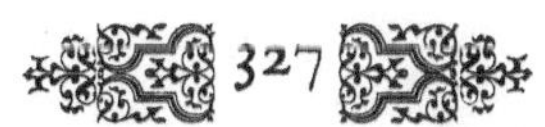

He put a hand on Louis' shoulder. 'Send me a telegram when you've reached Paris, won't you? I worry for you, Louis.'

'Say your rosary,' Albert's wife said. 'You have much to be thankful for.'

She closed the door of the carriage and let Albert walk Louis to the end of the platform.

'Another fifteen thousand, Louis. I'm not sure if I can do this anymore. I will try to see what I can do. Fifteen thousand is all I can do. Family ties and all.'

Louis smiled through his nervous tears.

'Thank you, Albert. I can buy us all passage to America if you'd like. You would like New York—the museums, the restaurants, the salons...'

'I'm sure they're just like the ones in Paris. And by that I mean that they're boring. Something to consider, no?' Albert replied.

He sat in the train car and watched Albert walk away into the dark.

When Albert's figure had at last disappeared into the

velvet black of the summer night, Louis Le Prince sat alone with himself and sighed deeply.

In the portfolio he had brought to Dijon to show Albert, he had brought the finished prints of that beautiful afternoon at Roundhay Cottage. He looked at them now as the photographs lay in his lap. A flood of memories filled him with longing and regret. A few warm tears escaped his tired eyes and he wiped them away, listlessly, not wanting to escape the delirium of the emotions he felt. He passed a gloved hand over Anne's image, as if to caress her in the frozen grey past. To have the light in her eyes again, to see her smile.

He closed his eyes again.

The train lurched forward.

There was a billow of steam against the star-pocked midnight blue of the late summer sky. Amid the glow of phosphorus sparks, in the soft caress of summer linen and the cold, wet autumn air, in the midst of fog and frost and the dust of the past—in a dizzying whirl of colors of landscapes of the past and present, in crowds along the Rue de Rivoli and at the Opéra—Louis dreamt. In his dreams, he floated up and away into the rarified cerulean and celandine and celadon of painterly skies. He felt the crunch of English gravel under his shoes and the smell of ivy and boxwood, felt the rustle of the rain-soaked privet.

Sereno

He unlatched an iron gate and walked down a slate path.

She was there—they all were. She had been waiting for him in the terrace at Roundhay.

Roundhay Garden Scene

Louis Le Prince disappeared on September 16, 1890.

His wife, Elizabeth Whitley Le Prince, called on Scotland Yard and the Gendarmerie to look for Louis. The search continued for some three years before finally going cold. He was declared legally dead in 1897.

Joseph Whitley arrived in America in 1891 to join Lizzie in looking for Louis. Amid soaring debts and in very poor health, he died the same year and was buried in New York City. Later, he was reburied next to Sarah Whitley in Leeds in 1894.

Anne 'Harriet' Hartley died in 1902.

Lizzie and Adolphe unsuccessfully sued Thomas Edison in 1893 for the patent for the motion picture camera. Adolphe testified in a later court case as a material witness against Edison and his company in another unrelated legal matter. Almost ten years to the day that Louis photographed his family at Roundhay, Adolphe was found dead of a shot to the head at Fire Island in New York.

The scene at Roundhay Garden is the oldest surviving motion picture in existence.

Sereno

About the author

JOE GALVÁN (1984—) is a writer, artist, composer and anthropologist. He was born in Harlingen, Texas, in the Rio Grande Valley of Texas. His work has appeared in *Texas Monthly, The Believer, Buckman, Deep Overstock, 1001*, and *Barrelhouse*.

Sereno was produced as part of the Certificate Program in Creative Writing at the Independent Publishing Resource Center in 2018.

He lives in Portland, Oregon.

Sereno